ANNO DOMINI

WES WILLETT

A WORK OF FICTION

An Anno Domini Publication

First published in The United States of America in 2017 by
Westley Willett.

10 9 8 7 6 5 4 3 2 1

Cover illustration by Justin Gerard.
Book design and layout by Leslie Henke - Frequency Design.

This is a work of fiction.

ISBN 978-0-578-19931-3

Learn more about Anno Domini on the Internet at
www.theinkforge.com

THE INKFORGE

ACKNOWLEDGMENTS

My heart is popping a seam while writing this. It's too full. I didn't know that writing down my thanks would be nearly this tough. To share gratitude with people who are part of a work that took over a decade to complete can be a bit tricky. Some people are not working with me anymore, while others have grown to be more like family. Some are family. All have been indispensable to this book.

So...

To my buddy, Brett McNew, thank you. You were in on this labor of love very early. Your writing inspires me and your friendship is the lifelong kind. Thank you.

To Becca McNew, the grammar geek: Thank you for always being willing to lend your knowledge to me. You and your family mean the world to me.

v

To Chris Rice. Your writing makes me jealous. You unwittingly taught me that joy is more important than perfectionism. Thank you for letting me bend your ear on those flights with random ideas and names for this book. Because of you, we have the High-Bourne.

To Cindy Morgan, you probably don't even realize what you did way back on that Christmas tour. Your interest in my writing gave me the courage to keep striving, to keep going. You did not have to take time for me, but you did. Someday, I hope that God will let me be that word of encouragement to someone, the way you were for me. Thank you.

To Crystal Bryant, the editing queen: Thank you for making the process as painless as possible. You didn't laugh or beat up an aspiring writer. You taught, adding just enough honey to make the medicine bearable. Thank you so much.

To Buddy Mullins, there is too much water under our bridges to put into simple thanks. Your interest toward my writing is always encouraging, but your family and friendship are one of God's sweetest graces to me.

To my sister, Angela, of this long list of talented friends, you are certainly amongst its most creative. Your belief in me and encouragement often kept me going. That is what a big sister does. That is what you did and still do. I love you.

To my brother, Mark, you're always there and always my bro. Whether it be music or books, you are there... I have no words.

To Michelle Hicks and Amy Jacobs, my Lifeway homeys:
(Amy's question): "What would you do if you didn't do what you do?"
(Wes' reluctant answer): "I would write stories... books."
That question, your interest, and consistent prompting was the adrenalin that finally pulled a manuscript out of me. Thank you both so much.

vii

To Luke, we did it buddy! Without you, I don't know if there would even be a book called Anno Domini, and I certainly know that it would not be what it is. Whatever comes of this work, whatever glory our God gets from it, is largely due to my knowing you. I may have held the pen, but so often you guided my hand. I can't express enough thanks for your friendship and influence.

To Melinda Leake and her 8th grade class of Heritage Middle School, Christian Leake, Andrew Holt, Chris Lanigan, Anna Coley, Abbey Bennett, Caitlin Avery, Stephanie Steiner, Kristiana Ingram: Thank you for enduring an early manuscript and for being some of my favorite alpha readers. Your input was valuable. There would not be a glossary without you!

To Don Emmit, thanks for all of the coffee and theology talks, and for letting me bend your ear about some of my wackier ideas on angels and demons. You make the notion of God's grace more tangible to me. Thank you.

To Mrs. Beth, the best lesson you have ever taught me is the one that never reached the stage – the kind of lesson that can only be lived out. You taught me what it looks like to desire God more than anything: To make my desire for his calling greater than my fear of failing. Thank you... I hope you see some of yourself in this book.

To April and Gracie, my two loves: You're always with me, loving me. Through tours, through pastoring, through writing books; still, you're there loving me. Not only would this book be less without you, I would be less of a man without you both in my life. I sure do love you.

# DEDICATIONS

I dedicate this book to my great God first. Every minute of every hour of every year spent writing this book is for Him. He transformed my fears into passions and has given me hinds feet for the high places I did not even know to ask for.

Then to all the Mal'aks out there with a calling bigger than you are: This book you hold in your hands has been such a calling for me. Let courage rise...

- Wes

CONTENTS

PROLOGUE:

"I know not why you wait, my Sovereign. Your prophets come no more, and for the better part of 400 years You have remained silent. Is there still hope for flesh, Great Lord of the Dawn? Is there hope for Adam's seed, so far from Eden? They are hunted like sheep by the Dark One, their bodies fuel for his war. A war not paid in blood, but in souls. God help me . . . human souls fill the margins of time and my own heart with a sorrow beyond the grasp of lamenting. I . . . am the Chronicler, Keeper of the Ages, Keeper of Sorrows. Long have they endured this abomination. Long have we, the High-Bourne of heaven, struggled to guard Your earthen treasures. How much longer, Father? Must we pity their children and spend our tears for fallen man? I am nothing if not your servant, Great Lord of the Light. It is to my honor that you have bestowed to me this duty that falls so heavily upon my quill. I am the Chronicler. . . . I record by your great power only truth in these dark days, my Lord . . . only truth. The pen itself will not let me write otherwise.

It carries Your will within it, but its weight is almost more than I can bear. Light help me, the war, Father . . . he is winning! Forgive me if I go too far. By your grace we will not fail your charge, Great Lord of lords. We of the High-Bourne will fight the Fallen One and his Baal spawn until eternity wanes. By Your word, we would soak the earth with the blood of our own for the children of Adam. But Father . . . I fear we cannot save them . . ."

A Song of Lament: Annals of the Chronicler . . . the 6ᵗʰ Age

CHAPTER 1:
CALLINGS

"Now is the time and the time is now." The words fell from Mal'ak's lips, barely a whisper, but crisp as morning air. "Light of the Dawn!" he said, his eyes popping open with a start. "Is it true? Am I really leaving *heaven?*" It sounded just as foreign coming out of his mouth as it had in his head. *Has anyone ever done that before? Certainly not a Ta'ow.*

"Crafters do not leave the Great Lord's Kingdom to go gallivanting about," he said, looking down his nose, in his best imitation of the Elders. "It just isn't done. Not since the Age of the Turning, anyway. We Ta'ow measure by the lines, we forge, we *build*. There has never been a *reason* for angels of our kind to *leave*."

Mal'ak rolled his eyes and sighed, peering outside the window to the white spires of the Great Lord's Kingdom. Shimmering stone walls rose from golden streets. Silver buttressed bridges spanned the clear living waters that were held aloft by arches forged from pure light—arches his Elders had forged. Mal'ak stared through it all. Was it just a dream? He took in a deep breath, uncertainty stirring the back corners of his mind while the rest of the space in his head swirled with excitement. He gazed at his home. The Pearl Gate came into focus, glimmering in the distance not far from his own room. It was his favorite. The single most beautiful gem in the kingdom, aside from the Great Lord's throne of course. Most mornings, Mal'ak found himself there, journal and quill in hand. Most mornings he would have already been at the Pearl by dawn. But this was not most mornings. Today, the dawn held the hint of something more. He could feel it under his skin. It was not loud, more like a still, small voice in his head. Suddenly, it whispered to him, '*Now is the time and the time is now!*' Mal'ak jerked, bumping his head hard on the windowsill. Quickly, he looked around the room to make sure he was still alone. "A Stirring whispered to me," he said, ears fidgeting. "By the Silver Cord! It's not a dream! A *Stirring* whispered to *me!*

"Mal'ak . . . Mal'ak," came a call just outside his window. Not bothering for the door, Mal'ak leaped through the window, five stories, out into the open air of heaven and nearly bowled Adam over onto the street. Deftly, Mal'ak hoisted Adam up, holding him eye level.

"Guess what Adam?" Mal'ak said, grinning. "*Now is the time and the time is now!*"

Adam chuckled, his feet dangling a good four feet above the ground. "Well, the time is always as the Great Lord says it is," Adam countered, gently patting Mal'ak's hands as if to say, "You can put me down now."

"I know, I know. Can you *feel* it, though? You can feel it too, right, the Stirring? It calls to me." Mal'ak's enthusiasm

3

seemed tied to his hands. Adam grunted, prying in vain at the sausage sized fingers wrapped around his waist, and laughed.

"Ok, ok. I suppose *now is the time and the time is now. Now for the Light*, put me down!"

Forgetting his own strength, Mal'ak whirled Adam into the air and roared, "I knew it! I knew it!" Adam came down on his backside with a grunt.

"Ahem. So . . . you felt the Stirring did you?" Adam winced, looking up from between Mal'ak's knees.

"Didn't everyone?" Mal'ak asked, his head bobbing.

"No, *everyone* did not. Stirrings are rare. The last one emptied the sacred halls themselves—you remember. Every High-Bourne sworn to the Lion Banner took to wing. They never came back, Mal'ak . . . . They are still there, on earth, Dawn shine upon them."

The fur on Mal'ak's neck bristled. *Light of the Dawn! Earth!* That place set his heart to pounding—that and the Stirring of course. A motion tugged at the corner of his eye. The Lion banner played on the breeze just above the city spires, solid red, with a golden lion's head that clearly marked this land a sovereign province of the King of all Kings. "A lion," Mal'ak whispered, his eyes still resting on the banner. "Adam, will I see a lion, a *real* earth lion, down there?" Mal'ak opened his mouth, baring his teeth, giving his best imitation of a lion.

"Well, it won't be the same, but sure." Adam shrugged, dusting himself off. "Just remember, *everything* is different there. Earth creatures are but echoes of the heavenly caste we have here in the kingdom of our Great Lord."

"Echoes?" Mal'ak smiled sidelong at Adam.

"Yes, but we need to stay focused. The Stirr—"

"Is there an echo of me, a *legend* about the Ta'ow?"

Hope brimmed so full in Mal'ak's white eyes that Adam thought it might just spill out if he didn't answer outright. Besides, ignoring the question would only be an invitation for Mal'ak's curiosity to drag his mind farther away from the point of their conversation than it already had.

"Well," Adam scratched his head. "There are bovine

creatures on earth called bulls or cows that would *kind of* be similar in appearance . . . I suppose. But Dawn's Light, Mal'ak, no human could ever mistake you for a cow." He pursed his lips at the notion. "Come to think of it, though, human myths have been influenced by the Ta'ow, to a certain extent—maybe even some of their *legends*," he said with a wink.

"Really?" Mal'ak's eyes grew to the size of saucers.

"*Minotaur* . . ." Adam nodded. "Yes, Minotaur is what they called your kind, if memory serves me. I suppose Heaven can't help but touch the world of man now and again. If I were a betting man, I'd wager they're responsible for most, if not all of man's legends." Adam looked up into Mal'ak's eyes and they were blank as river stone. *The Dawn only knows where he was off to this time. Probably petting an earth lion somewhere, or fighting in glorious battle with High-Bourne against the Dragon lord himself.* Compassion touched Adam's eyes as he watched Mal'ak. *Light of the Dawn, he's gifted*, Adam thought. *That is for certain. Naive, and completely*

out of his depth. That is also for certain. "Callings." Adam puffed the word through the bangs of his hair with a long sigh. "Yeah . . . I'd say you're almost perfect for one."

"What? Wait, you think I'm not ready?

Adam's cheeks colored. He'd not realized, he'd been thinking out loud. "Not ready?" Adam let his concern dissolve into a smile. "Of course you're not ready, you big ox. Nobody is ready for their Calling. So you're perfect! This has the Great Lord's fingerprints all over it."

"You think so?" Mal'ak laughed out loud.

"Tailor made, by the Dawn Bringer himself, I'd say."

Mal'ak beamed at Adam's approval, nearly blushing right through his chestnut coat. He never had known what to do with a proper compliment as long as Adam had known him.

"This journey Mal'ak, *your* journey, is a Calling to be sure, make no mistake. Stirrings always are. This will be an adventure never to be *forgotten.*" Adam's tone shifted with the last word. He tried to hide it, but Mal'ak could sense the tightness in his voice. "You must listen closely.

7

The Blight, what humans call sin?"

Mal'ak nodded.

"On earth, you will run into certain *situations*—things you have never seen before, more importantly things you have never felt before, because of this Blight." Adam's brow pulled inward, his eyes glistening. "I cannot prepare you for this. The Dawn knows, I wish I could. But that is exactly what a journey does, you know." A smile touched the left side of his lips, but didn't quite connect to his eyes. "It prepares through experience, and your *Calling* steels you in that experience—in those moments when you need most."

"Prepares me for what?" Mal'ak asked, wide eyed.

"The earth, Mal'ak. It is fallen. Its rightful lords are one of the reasons for the fall. *I* . . . am one of those reasons."

"But the Dragon lord—" Mal'ak protested.

"Yes, the Dragon." Adam shushed him with an open hand. "That is exactly where the Dragon lord is, Sheol's flames burn him and his Blight." Adam paused as if measuring his words, then squared his gaze on Mal'ak.

Chapter 1: Callings

"Do you know what Sacrosanct means?" He searched the whites of Mal'ak's eyes for a flicker of understanding. "It is magic—*high* magic that predates the Ages themselves. The Great Lord is on the move, Mal'ak. It is *He* that wills and it is *He* that binds you to this Calling, to something larger than yourself, larger than us all. This kind of magic cannot not be stopped, even by shadow spawn. It means that when you leave here, you will go with more than the propitious smiles of heaven at your back. You will go with the force of *His* will. Mal'ak . . . it means that you *will* succeed in your calling!"

"Yes!" Mal'ak said triumphantly.

Adam hesitated, adding softly, "But it does not mean that your journey will be safe. Stirrings and Callings are many things to be sure, but Callings are never, ever safe— especially when bound by Sacrosanct. Do you understand?"

Mal'ak heard most of what Adam was saying, but couldn't help himself. One piece of the conversation paled everything else to non-importance as far as he was concerned. "Sac-ro-sanct?" He slowly pronounced each syllable, while both bushy eyebrows climbed up his forehead. "The *Great Lord* sent *you* to talk to *me?*"

Adam's face softened. "I told you . . . it is your Calling. If I know of your love for earth, would the Great Lord not know as well? Who do you think seeded that passion inside of you?" He winked with a sly grin.

"So . . . His will *is* my Calling?" Mal'ak asked in astonishment.

"Yeah, His will, your calling."

Mal'ak mumbled something about time and space, and then a question shot from his mouth like an arrow. "What is it like, Adam?

Adam cocked a brow upward. "What do mean?"

"You know, what is it like to be in a place where the Great Lord . . . well, *moves?*" Mal'ak arched a wide sweeping motion with his hands, trying to explain. "Here, in Heaven, He just *is* and, and in His nearness we *are,* but down there, oh, Adam!" Mal'ak knuckled his head quizzically. "Down there, everything is still, sort of *becoming,* isn't it? Isn't that what time does? It becomes? The Great Lord brushes His fingertips through the Deep of the Narrows, His touch reaches the earth and in His wake life moves, *time* moves— why, I've never even felt time before . . . ." His words trailed off, bushy ears fidgeting as the moment sank into them both.

"Preparations have already been made, Mal'ak. Please, listen closely now. No more daydreaming. There is one last thing you need know my friend: you will carry a Summons."

"A Summons?" Mal'ak blinked. "What kind of—"

"This kind." Adam held out two smooth stones, one in each hand.

Mal'ak swallowed hard. "Those are Oracles, Adam— Light! Two of them!"

"Yes, they're Summoning Stones," Adam said, holding them at eye level. Mal'ak wasn't sure if he should stare, or look away out of respect. He did not want to appear nosy. Ta'ow were *not* nosy. Some might say he had a *well-rounded* curiosity, but never nosy.

"What do they do?" he asked, his voice a little more

eager than he'd hoped for.

"You'll know when the time comes," Adam said flatly, sliding the two stones inside of Mal'ak's pack. "I'm sorry, I cannot tell you any more than I already have." Adam pulled out a folded long cloak made from Silver Weave from under his own—it had an oversized cowl.

"My cloak," Mal'ak said, surprised.

"You'll need to put this on." Adam held it out expectantly, arm holes open. "I knew it was your favorite so I took the liberty of preparing it for you—it has been Warded for your journey."

"Warded?" Mal'ak slid his arms into the soft weave of his cloak. "Why does it have to be Warded?"

Adam held up one hand, cutting him off in mid-sentence. "Your remaining questions will have to be answered by your journey," he said with a smile. "Halo waits for you, Mal'ak, even now, and so does your Calling. Remember all that we have spoken of. Now, you must go. *The Dawn shine upon you, and keep you.*" With these words, a large white circlet of light appeared seven cubits in front of them both.

Mal'ak hesitated for a moment, speechless. He had wondered what this day would be like—waited so long for a moment like this, and somehow, the moment was waiting on him now.

"You already have everything you need for the journey. Mal'ak . . . you were made for this moment," Adam said gently.

Mal'ak's eyes widened, and a toothy grin nearly split his face in half.

"You know what Adam? *This* is my brand new favorite day."

Adam's ancient eyes looked deep into Mal'ak's. *"Now is the time, and the time is now,* old friend. There is your Calling, Mal'ak . . . . Go get it!"

Mal'ak reached out his hand. Halo's arch trembled before him. For a moment, he just stared, letting his hand hover above it. It burned so evenly, so pure. One touch is all it would take. He glanced up to the Lion banner waving proudly above the white spires of heaven, then slowly, he let his eyes fall to Adam, dropped his hand and was gone.

CHAPTER 2:
ELISHEBA

Mal'ak pushed up from the ground, opening his eyes. Dirt and sulfur caked his nostrils. He could not recall how or when he landed. All he could remember was the arch of Halo racing under his fingertips and the incredible rush of trans-luminance speed hurtling his body forward into the time stream. *Time!* thought Mal'ak. He breathed in, sniffing the air anxiously, letting his senses stretch outward. He could feel it. He could actually feel time move.

Suddenly, hellfire smashed into the earth, cratering the ground, not more than fourteen cubits from where he stood. Flames plumed into the air, leaving the stench of sulfur and bile. Rivulets of molten rock snaked down the crater's rim. His stomach lurched. Vomit stung the back of his throat and he swallowed hard, trying to keep it down. The red haze of earth rushed into focus and the smell of demon was everywhere. Mal'ak clamored beside a scorched boulder to the left of the crater's edge. He strained upwards, catching glimpses of flittering shapes high above. Angels strobed before his eyes, in full view one moment, gone the next. Demons, thick as flies, covered the red Haze of earth's sky. "Legion—Dragon spawn!" he whispered. He covered his ears but could still hear them clashing in mid-air with the Shade of His Hand, the High-Bourne of heaven.

"By the Silver Cord!" he muttered. Adam had tried to explain, but Mal'ak was simply not prepared for this. How could he be? Bodies fell from the sky by the hundreds, cratering the ground, one punching a hole in the dirt right beside him. His gut clenched in a knot. *Was the body in that hole of sunken earth High-Bourne or Legion?*

18

CHAPTER 2: ELISHEBA

Mal'ak jumped with a start as all of a sudden the ground beneath him tilted vertically. Stumbling backward, he slid off the edge of something that scraped against his hooves like bone scraping against metal. Heat rippled the air, revealing a single wing that had been right under him. "By the Dawn!" Mal'ak said, stepping back. Disbelief widened his snowy eyes. He had walked right on top of the thing without even knowing. "Invisible," he muttered. "It must have been." Invisible wings, but hard as flint. Goggle-eyed, he watched them change right before him, and the slender face of an angel peered from underneath the ivory plating of her wings. Mal'ak's eyes fell to the symbol of the Lion banner on her tunic and his heart soared. "High-Bourne," he shouted.

She sprang with feline grace and strength that was uncanny for one so small. Her hands blurred, catching the nape of his cloak, and with one quick jerk, she yanked his seven cubit frame to the ground. It actually hurt. A little, anyway.

"Who are you?" she spat, scanning the sky. Her eyes,

like golden embers, reminded Mal'ak of a sunrise. She never let her gaze rest on him for more than a moment though, watching above, below and all around him, while her head turned in an odd sweeping motion. A buzzing sound came from her mouth. It took Mal'ak a moment to understand; she was speaking words. Words uttered almost too fast to be understood. Mal'ak could tell she was unaware that she was speaking so fast, not to mention that head motion thing she kept doing over and over. Apparently, it all seemed normal conversation to her. She had not let go of the nape of his cloak, which was sort of choking him.

"I asked you a question, Ta'ow." She glared as if he were taking far too long to answer. "Did the Great Lord send you? Are there more? More . . . Ta'ow?" She paused, red coloring the cheeks of that otherwise cool High-Bourne face. Mal'ak knew she meant no offense. He watched her brow bend inward trying to make sense of why reinforcements would be Ta'ow and not something more formidable. *No wonder she's shocked*, he thought, slightly embarrassed. *Ta'ow are strong, but we don't even have wings.* Now it was his turn to flush. He hoped his chestnut coat hid the heat in his cheeks.

"I . . . I'm alone," Mal'ak blurted. "Oh, and I carry a message! From the Great Lord," he managed. Her eyes grew wider with his last four words.

"You carry a message for us?" Her grip somehow managed to increase in pressure with the question. Mal'ak grunted slightly. Hellfire punched another hole in the ground behind them; she blinked like it never happened and his words alone were all that mattered now.

"What is our Lord's message? Please, Ta'ow, you must make haste!"

Mal'ak fumbled for the right pocket of his favorite pack, trying to keep up with the insane pace of events. He pulled the Summoning Stones from the bottom pocket, shooting them toward her, one in each hand.

"Oh! And my calling is Sacrosanct," he added triumphantly.

"Anathema!" The High-Bourne recoiled, jerking away from the stones like Mal'ak held Dragon spawn in each hand. Now it was *she* who seemed to be wrestling with the pace of their conversation. She repeated the word 'Sacrosanct' with a reverence worthy of the Lion Banner, her eyes darting from the Summoning Stones in his hands, then skyward and back again. Her mouth however, continued in a blur of words, too quick to understand—a one sided conversation with herself, while her eyes continued that sweeping motion skyward. *Something about being aligned with the Quintessence.* Mal'ak knew of the legend of the Quintessence, but had never seen it before. Suddenly, her golden eyes leveled on him in a blend of excitement and horror.

"By the Silver Cord—do you know what those are, Ta'ow? Do you know what this means?" she whispered, pulling him close enough to feel the breath from her mouth. "The Epoch Horizon!"

Mal'ak's concern for her was rising. The marble features of her face were smooth but somehow drawn

22

taught. "We must reach the Chronicler," she said frantically. "He will know what to do."

It wasn't until this moment that Mal'ak noticed the long slender blade in her other hand. It came out of the backside of her gauntleted fist. It wasn't pointed at him but her eyes were glazed wide open with something he had never seen before—something alien that did not exist in the Great Lord's Kingdom, but somehow he recognized it very, very clearly—*fear*. He wasn't sure how he recognized it. Instinct maybe? The feeling was primal though, and oddly like something he had forgotten. Mal'ak was about to speak when his eye caught the gleam of liquid tracing the edge of her elbow. Essence bled down her arm, mixing between her fingers, coloring the hilt of the blade in her hand red. A slow, steady stream dripped from the tip of her blade, pooling on the ground. Mal'ak swallowed hard. He had never seen anyone *bleed* before, and for some reason his pulse began to quicken. He knew better than to believe her weak, he knew by the iron grip she held him in, but still, she seemed so helpless, bleeding like that.

"My name is Elisheba," she said through clenched teeth, her whole body shuddering with the words.

"You are in pain," Mal'ak said, leaning in against her fists still clutching his cowl. All at once, her iron grip collapsed without resistance. The wound was worse than he'd imagined. Her other wing—the one she had been lying on—was almost ripped in half from the top down. Another thing Mal'ak wasn't used to seeing . . . pain. Mal'ak couldn't help himself. He ignored her blade, and for the moment, completely forgot there was a war going on. Mal'ak's heart was suddenly set on fire by the instinct to help her and before he knew it, he was running with her in his arms. He did not remember picking her up, and he had no clue where he was running to. He just ran. *Anywhere but here,* he thought. The shock on her ageless face was a mixture of horror and fear.

"What are you doing?" she half yelled, trying to keep her voice down. "They'll see us," she shouted as much as a whisper would allow. "There are Dragon about." She glanced from his face to the sky, her eyes a rapid fire of movement. "I don't want to hurt you, Ta'ow, but if you don't put me down, you'll get us both killed!"

He felt the blade from her gauntlets against his throat now.

"Please . . . don't make me hurt you," she said, her voice pulled tight with strain but the truth of her words obvious in her tone—she was *not* bluffing. Her eyes were fire and her face might have been marble mounted within starless night. She was beautiful. He slowed his gait as her blade drew the smallest trickle of essence from his throat. "From the Great Lord's Kingdom or no, you *will* put me down, Ta'ow."

"My name is Mal'ak," he said, stopping at the edge of a crater, still holding her in his arms. "Please—I want to help you."

CHAPTER 3: TANNIN

All of a sudden, darkness descended, a living darkness that seemed to swallow the sun. His arms were suddenly empty. Elisheba danced about the darkness, jumping, flipping, dipping with blinding speed, stabbing into the darkness ferociously. Her advances were so graceful she seemed at dance with her own blades. Her face was stone etched fury, and on oath, he couldn't tell if she was growling or singing. Her dance met the darkness, her blades a whirring blur, whistling out death songs. Chunks of demon hide and severed limbs fell lifeless to the ground.

The glow of Halo appeared above her head, pushing back the dark, and it dawned on Mal'ak that they now stood in her aura alone, that her small circlet of light was all that was keeping the darkness at bay, a darkness that moved of its own accord. It surrounded them, whispering the abominations it would do to them when her little light was extinguished. Suddenly, she went to one knee. Essence caked around her fingers, pooling at her feet. She was bleeding out, but she continued to fight. 'I am nearly expired, Mal'ak of the Ta'ow,' came her voice in his head. He realized, she hadn't spoken from her mouth, but opened a link that connected their minds. He could *feel* her mind. The sensation was unlike anything he had ever felt before—open, more intimate than mere friendship. He could feel her pain, her exhaustion, and a steel core under that porcelain veneer, forged by a millennia of war. She held no fear of death, not for herself. Her trepidation was for him; for the mission.

'Today, I will earn a new name, Ta'ow!' Her determination pulsed through the link.

A new name? thought Mal'ak.

"Finish your calling Ta'ow! It is Sacrosanct, you cannot fail—you will *not* fail!" She did not scream as the darkness swallowed her whole. She only starred at him with a fiery gleam in her eyes and said, *"My life for yours, your life for mine. Honor and Strength . . . for the KING!"* That was the last thing he remembered before unconsciousness.

When his eyes popped open, it was dark, but a different kind of darkness—the unmoving, un-living kind. He was obviously not on the battlefield anymore. Maybe underground, it was hard to be sure. After a moment, his eyes adjusted and he almost wished they hadn't. An immense winged monster took shape in the shadows, and demons crawled from floor to ceiling of a cavernous room. Moans seemed to come from the corridors lining the walls and holes in the ceiling, but he could not pinpoint exactly where the suffering was coming from. It seemed to be coming from everywhere.

"My name is Tannin," the winged monster said.

His voice was thunder echoing across the stone dampness of the cavern. Mal'ak peered through the darkness with a quick once over of his own body, which revealed that he was unharmed. But—Elisheba! His eyes scanned the room again. She was nowhere to be found.

"Where is she? Where is Elisheba?" Mal'ak blurted without thinking.

"She isss . . . *busy*." The archdemon's lips curled in sneer that sent chills down Mal'ak's spine. The demon's accent drawled out in slow serpent-like patience. Tannin leaned in so close, Mal'ak could smell the sulfurous bile of his breath.

"Tannin's eyes are upon you speck. Speak or be devoured," the Dragon said.

Mal'ak had never seen a Dragon this close before. He tried not to imagine how many angels this vile creature had already eaten.

"I will not tell you again, Ta'ow."

Mal'ak rubbed his throat. It was raw, like he'd

swallowed an entire loaf of prickleberry bread and chased it down with a pitcher of sulfur. His heart beat like his chest would explode, but something inside of him rose up. He met Tannin's gaze flatly and held it without so much as a blink. "I am Taur Mal'akim of the Ta'ow."

It came out without him even meaning to. Tannin's head cocked to one side. Mal'ak could almost see the great Dragon's mind turning his words around from every direction, every angle, taking his measure of him in the process. He also discerned a hint of uncertainty in the ancient demon's face. Mal'ak opened his mouth again. "I come in the Name of He Who Brings the Dawn, and my summons is Sacrosanct." The name "He Who Brings the Dawn" stirred a frenzy of veiled whispers and hushed growls in the cavernous room. It wasn't until now, Mal'ak realized he was aglow.

Dawn's Light! When did that happen? Mal'ak thought, swallowing hard.

"Sacrosssanct?" Tannin backed away casually,

dragging out the word with that distinct reptilian drawl. Mal'ak could sense Tannin's uncertainty by the measure of his movements. The distance between the elongated stride was too purposeful. The quickening speed and nervous flicking of the tail. He had never used his gift as a Crafter to measure something's movement. But then again, he had never been in a Dragon's lair before either.

The room was almost clear of Legion now, with the exception of a few rows of eyes peering at him out of holes in the ceiling and from under the cover of shadow.

"You come into *my* stronghold and dare speak *His* name, claiming the ancient right of Sacrosssanct, here? You glow with power that is not your own, and yet you have no wings to even speak of?" Tannin chuckled a low rumble that Mal'ak felt through the stone floor beneath. It blended in with the constant moaning and suffering of this place in a way that made Mal'ak's fur bristle. "We have ourselves an enigma, my Legion. Little Ta'ow, you are either what you say you are or you are insane. Tell me quickly, *meat*, before I tire of you, what *is* your summonsss?"

Mal'ak reached into his pocketed pack that was somehow still hanging just beneath the folds of his cloak. He couldn't believe it was still there, but then again, the Legion didn't seem too keen on being near him—much less touching him. He felt the two smooth stones at the very bottom of the pouch. Gripping only one, he shot his hand out, letting it sit in the flat of his palm, dull and smooth. It had the look of a river stone, but clear, with greenish hues and a single rune etched into its smooth surface. Tannin's eyes grew a quarter in size.

"A Summoning Stone!" the Dragon's words seemed to reveal more astonishment than even Elisheba's response.

Mal'ak opened his mouth again. "Let all under heaven and earth, Thrones, Dominions, Principalities, and Powers, *all* creatures tethered to the Silver Cord, answer the call of the Epoch Horizon."

Mal'ak recognized his own voice but he knew it was not him talking. Tannin eased a couple more steps away, and was for the moment lost in thought. His saucer sized eyes twitched with what looked like concern and the corners slanted toward anger.

"Rebuked in my own stronghold, by an insignificant Crafter, claiming the ancient right of Sacrosssanct? Summoning *all* creatures to this—*Epoch Horizon?*" The last words dripped from his mouth with sarcasm. Tannin's gaze narrowed. He easily reached across the distance of the cavern, snatching the Summoning Stone from Mal'ak's palm. It happened almost too fast for Mal'ak to see. Tannin turned it end upon end.

"It *is* real," he said, with a ring of unbelief in his voice. "This is madness," he spat. "*You* come to *me* with ancient rights and a summons from the Great Lord? *You?* Tell me, little Ta'ow, do you even know what the Summoning Stones are for? Do you know where they lead?" He didn't give Mal'ak the chance to answer before he hissed, "They lead to the Deep of the Narrows, you trifling little speck. And do you know what dwells in the Deep of the Narrows, Mal'ak of the Ta'ow?" He looked at Mal'ak, and this time, he waited. When Mal'ak gave no answer, Tannin roared in laughter.

"Of course you don't. They never told you, did they? *My call is Sacrosssanct.*" Tannin's voice was sheer mockery. This brought jeers from the few demons bold enough to laugh from the shadows.

"You are a fool, Ta'ow. The Great Lord has abandoned this world and all the Flesh-Walkers on it.

"*We* rule this Godless planet. The Legion rule flesh, and we have had our way with them for more than four hundred years." Tannin quirked a sneer. "*Now* He summons? *Now* He calls to us? And for what? And why in Sheol's flames would I *ever* take the word of a stinking Ta'ow like you? Why should *I* bring meat like you to the attention of my masters?"

Mal'ak stood straight, the hair bristling just below the back of his head at the tip of his spine. He didn't fully understand what was happening, but that same feeling filled him again, overriding the fear in his gut, that new emotion he was just getting familiar with. He felt his hands ball into fists and his heart pound the insides of his chest. He opened his mouth with words that were again, clearly not his own. "Your belief is irrelevant, Dragon. All that is required of you and your masters is obedience. But if faith you lack, then know this, He Who Brings the Dawn never changes. His will is sovereign, and His call *will* bind all by the ancient right of Sacrosanct. Tell your masters that *all* . . . must pass through the Narrows, and *all* shall pass unmolested, so long as essence be not spilled."

Tannin knew for certain that what any Ta'ow or High-Bourne said must be true if indeed his allegiance was to the Lion Banner. He also knew that this Ta'ow was much more than what he seemed. But what struck Tannin the most at the moment was one small word he had somehow overlooked earlier. Tannin's eyes lingered upon the ancient Summoning Stone in his hand, before steadying his gaze upon Mal'ak.

"*All*," he said slowly, the corner of his lips sliding

up, revealing two rows of fangs long enough to make good on his earlier promise. "You said *all*, Ta'ow. Does *all* include High-Bourne as well? Does it include you?"

"Yes," Mal'ak said flatly.

"Well now, that changes things, doesn't it." Tannin's sneer grew even wider. "*All*, meaning Legion *and* High-Bourne . . . *All* must pass through the Narrows, and *all* will pass through unmolested, so that *all* can witness the Great Lord's 'Epoch Horizon,' so long as essence is not spilled?"

"You have my word." Mal'ak nodded.

"*Your word?*" Tannin broke into laughter. "Who would dare to spill essence in the Narrows?" he asked contemptuously, his face innocent, or as innocent as a Dragon's face could be. Suddenly, Tannin leaned in close to Mal'ak, eclipsing the entire room, his whisper cutting through the air like a blade.

"You reek of holiness, Ta'ow, so I *know* your word is good. But why not give us a demonstration? Hmm? Yesss, let us see this *summons* in action, shall we? A 'good gesture,' as the Flesh-Walkers say, for those of us . . . *lacking* in faith?"

Mal'ak moved to protest, but was too late. In the blink of an eye, Tannin swung the stone down hard upon the cavern floor.

Tiiing!

The stone rang a mellifluous sound through the air, high in pitch, almost like crystal. A portal tore open almost on top of them both. The cascading sound of water fell on Mal'ak's ears, like the sound of a thousand waterfalls, drowning out the ting and everything else. Even the unceasing moans heard in this place were swallowed up by the deluge. Tannin held the Summoning Stone high above his head. His fingers trembled, leaking a greenish glow connected to the portal. Fear was evident in the demon's eyes now, though he was trying his best to hide it. He was backing away. They stood for a moment, completely alone before the portal's raging mouth now. No words passed between them, or could. Mal'ak gazed into the Deep of the Narrows—a portal black as the abyss, his own distorted reflection looking back at him. His heart pounded the sides of his chest. A tug of war, of heart and mind, between this new emotion he now hated, called fear, and that deep longing Adam said would steel him through this journey– the calling of his King. His mind went to Elisheba and he knew that somewhere deep inside of him the decision was already made, the message just hadn't reached his limbs yet. Mal'ak knew if there were any glimmer of hope for survival for him or Elisheba, it lay somewhere on the other side of that portal. He never looked back to Tannin, and without a word, collided with his own reflection into the roaring Deep of the Narrows.

CHAPTER 4: THE DEEP OF THE NARROWS

A chill slid over his skin, and his breath caught. Even through his chestnut coat, the cold was shocking. The ground beneath him fell away and the world went white as he tumbled. By the time Mal'ak recognized the ground, he had already smashed into it. Cold rushed in from all sides, filling his ears and burning his eyes. Blinking and spitting, Mal'ak opened his mouth to take in a breath and immediately his mouth crackled. The air froze around the moisture of his tongue. Frozen droplets blanketed the thick layers of his coat in tiny sparkles that formed icicles at his elbows. He shook his head, trying to blink away the fogginess and the Narrows spread out before him, endless and frozen. Ice peaks rose in the distance out of a dead fog, maybe mountains, he wasn't sure. At this distance, they bore an uncanny resemblance to waves rather than mountains—giant frozen waves. But he knew that was ridiculous. Of course, it was no more ridiculous than what loomed above him. He spun a full circle, just to be sure he was seeing correctly. A frozen ocean stood above him and another frozen ocean below him. He stood in the space between. There were no connecting sides to speak of as far as he could tell. Of course, it might be attributed to the fog. Then again, even if there were sides, that still did not explain what held that ocean of water far above his head. *Maybe there was a way out. Maybe the way leading out lay just beyond the fog. Or . . . maybe I am just lost between two strange oceans in a place that give Dragons the willies.* He grimaced. *There must be a way out. Callings do not come without doors,* he thought resolutely. *What would Adam do?*

CHAPTER 4: THE DEEP OF THE NARROWS

He paced around in the knee-deep ice and snow, trying to think, but kept getting distracted by the way the ice sounded when it crunched under his hooves. *Such a marvelous crunch,* he thought. Suddenly, a ledge seemed to appear from out of nowhere. He bowed up, hunching his shoulders forward, his arms working in frantic circles, trying to keep himself on the ledge. A hole—no, a cavernous abyss spread out before him. He teetered precariously on a warm breeze, the wind whipping at his fur, folding his ears back. Balancing on the ledge, he held his breath, and took one large, wobbly step backward, then collapsed. *The Dawn's favor be upon me, that was close!* he thought. *Where did that thing come from? It was suddenly just there! Or was I suddenly just . . . distracted?* Mal'ak's cheeks felt warm. Even though there was no one around to see it, he was embarrassed.

"Concentrate, Mal'ak!" he chided himself. "You cannot afford to lose yourself in curious baubles and every passing snowflake. This place will kill you."

The hole had not been hiding, and it certainly

did not leap out in front of him. It just blended into the landscape—white, like everything else in the Narrows. So there was no real danger—not really. *Well . . . unless you don't pay attention and fall into it,* he thought ominously. It did seem embarrassingly obvious *now.* From the ledge, it dominated the landscape, a deep flat hole, bore into a frozen ocean, like the sea had opened its mouth and frozen in place. No icicles hung from the cave's mouth, though. It was strangely smooth and glassy along the interior, like something had melted right through it. He could only imagine the Summoning Stone must have bored it out that way when he came through from Tannin's lair. As cold as it was here, it probably refroze instantly. Dawn's Light, what else could it have been? There was nothing else here. He looked around for a light source, but the ice seemed to have a source all its own—a far glow, in the distance. How far, he could not tell. The sheer size of this place left Mal'ak feeling small. He supposed that entire cities could fit within the hollows of where he stood right now.

44

CHAPTER 4: THE DEEP OF THE NARROWS

At least it is safe here, he thought. The portal was gone and, judging by the look on Tannin's face, he would not have to worry about being followed. *Light of the Dawn! What could make a Dragon so fearful?* Mal'ak shivered in spite of himself. Being of the celestial caste, cold was not usually a problem, but the cold here somehow crept past his fur and into his bones. He scratched his neck thoroughly, knuckling all the way up to his chin hair. So many new sensations to catalog. And he seemed to have developed an itch. *Is this normal?* he thought, as he scratched and scratched and scratched. *Light*!

"Itch scratching is *great*." He chuckled. "I bet Flesh-Walkers do it all the time." He *had* to write about this as soon as he left this dismal place. *I can't wait to tell Adam. More human all the time.* He grinned.

Only one direction was feasible, really. The gargantuan hole carved into the ice looming ahead of him. It dropped dangerously where he stood, but forty cubits to the right, the hole looked slanted enough to walk down into without falling. It could be a passage for a deep spring that remained unfrozen far under the ice. And that meant an outlet had to be somewhere ahead. Mal'ak liked a clear direction, even if that direction was the result of few other options. He picked up his pack and shimmied over to the navigable ledge to his right. Sliding belly first, he eased over the lip, into the cave's mouth, onto smooth clear ice. It was slippery, but he managed well enough. His hooves made little divots along the cave wall as he climbed downward, and he created simple hand holds by forcing his fingers into the solid ice. *Not bad for a Crafter.* He smiled. After a while of climbing, the pitch of the cave floor leveled off a bit. It was still steep, but level enough for Mal'ak to hold a steady gait if he ran. So he ran, and ran, and ran. He ran until his feet ached from pounding the ice. Eventually he lost all sense of direction and how long he had been running, though truthfully, it did not seem to matter much. In the white of the Narrows, nothing seemed to change no matter how far he ran, except for the melting ice. That was the definitive change that kept him running this long and not turning around. The deeper he went, the thinner the ice became. He thought he was imagining it at first, but he could feel the warmth of a thermal blowing through the cave, and the ice was definitely melting. He could actually see through the frozen water to darker liquid beneath. It was black and churned a bubbling rage of current underneath. He could not figure out how white ice could come from black water, but that was just another item in a long list of mysteries that seemed to keep mounting in the Narrows. The frost on his fur had melted, leaving him ice-free but soaked, steam rising from his body and mouth. *At least I'm not freezing anymore*, he thought. Not far ahead, the tunnel ended abruptly, the ice forming a thinning shoreline that dropped straight into deep water. To Mal'ak's amazement, the water above was *completely* unfrozen. It churned with unnatural movement, stirring rather than flowing. Only the ice he stood on and behind him remained frozen, and even that was melting fast. Mal'ak had no idea how long he had run through the white of the Narrows. It could have been hours, maybe days. It was impossible to say. Truth was, it didn't matter, as long as it was far from Tannin. He looked around, scratching that marvelous itch.

It was downright strange, that water above him. And even more strange was the thinning ice he stood on. It had thinned to the point that he was *sure* he should have fallen through, but his hooves rested on the thinning ice, just as if he were standing on the celestial streets back home. There was nowhere left to run. Any further and he would have to swim, and Dawn knows, he wasn't crazy about that idea.

Surely I'm beyond Tannin's stronghold by now, he thought. He would not have traveled this far, but he had to be absolutely sure he would not step out of the Narrows only to fall into Tannin's hands again. Mal'ak pulled the other Summoning Stone from his pack. The rune atop its surface perfectly mirrored the one he had left with Tannin. It was the Old Tongue—a rare and tiny portion of the divine language. It was only used by the most gifted of the celestial caste. Strangely, it was not an entire word, but only an utterance.

"By the Silver Cord," he muttered. "Names confer power, but so much power in one utterance?" If a single utterance alone carved a giant ice hole into the Narrows, what would manifest if the rest of the word could be spoken?

His understanding the Old Tongue was limited. The language itself lay hidden somewhere within the cipher of a divine melody. But what was the melody? He loved to sing. There was a lot of that going on under the Lion banner. His cheeks spread into a smile as he softly hummed the melodies of his homeland. He missed Adam—he missed . . . *Dawn Bringer's Light.* He shook his head. Homesickness—another alien emotion that never happened in the Great Lord's Kingdom. He would write that down, too. Just as soon as he was away from this place. But right now, he had to get out of here. Elisheba was depending on him. Every minute he spent here was another minute she had to spend in Tannin's lair. *What were they doing to her?* Chills ran up his spine. No, he could not let himself dwell on that. Not now, not here.

Staring at the stone, an idea came to him. His fingers

traced the hewn out curve of the single rune atop the stone's smooth surface and he noticed something. The bottom of the stone was concave. It was subtle, but underneath, it curved inward in a shallow bowl fashion. Remembering the way in which Tannin had struck the other stone to manifest the portal, Mal'ak raised the Summoning Stone above his head, and with a quick flick of his wrist, he struck it against the side of his hoof. *Tiiiing*, it chimed like a crystal sings, and felt warm in his hand—*really* warm. The ancient rune lit with a green glow along its surface. Whispers from a forgotten age grew in Mal'ak's ear—an utterance, alien but somehow familiar, took form in the back of his mind. It was divine, and felt almost natural, more like a forgotten melody than a broken language. He gasped. It was flawless! He wondered if Tannin had heard it, too. The droning was only a fraction of a word but it was encased in that flawless melody. Mal'ak could only guess the meaning, but there it was, singing in his head. Immediately, a portal roared open behind him. It startled him so, he pitched forward onto the open water.

CHAPTER 4: THE DEEP OF THE NARROWS

Mal'ak's instinct was to hold his breath and close his eyes. He shot his arm above his head to keep the Summoning Stone from being submerged, but there was no need—no splash, no black sea to slowly drown him, no anything. He cracked one eye open and found himself sprawled atop the surface of the black waters; Summoning Stone held in one hand, teeming with green energy, connected to the portal, and his other hand pressed flat against the surface of the water as if it were solid. Faintly, a glow along the lining of his oversized cowl revealed a ward that had been woven in.

"Adam," he whispered, with a grin. Probably another reason Tannin had kept his distance—and as well he did, Mal'ak thought, relieved. Dragons were among the highest in the celestial caste. One such as Tannin would have sensed the wards presence on his cowl for sure. Slowly, Mal'ak's relief firmed into surprise. Surprise at the providence of such an odd warding, and how perfectly attuned it was to his needs. First inside Tannin's stronghold and now here, in this place.

He had never stood on water before; the tottering sensation felt a bit unsteady, but he got to his feet easy enough. Under him lay a bottomless abyss with a thin film of surface tension, thanks to the magic of Adam's Ward. It was all that kept him from plunging into the depths. He turned to face the portal roaring fiercely behind him. Suddenly, heat to match any of his kilns back home surged up from the dark waters beneath him. The landscape melted before him like candle wax—the cave, the path . . . all of it gone. Mal'ak's eyes broadened as he starred into the briny darkness beneath him. *Dawn's Light.* That water was churning hot, and getting hotter by the second. He rubbed his eyes, blinking over and over, trying to comprehend what was coming into focus. But it did not make sense, or he didn't want it to. He took a step backward and arched his head to one side, blinking again and . . . .

"By the Silver Cord!" He choked back a scream. His hooves puckered the surface as he stood atop the murky blackness. The Narrows beneath him boiled like a cauldron.

Only the thin surface of Adam's Ward stood between him and a large circular shape taking form underneath him. A yellow-slitted eye, sixteen cubits in diameter, was staring at him through the blackness. It dwarfed anything Mal'ak had ever seen before. If not for the Ward on his cloak, he might have fallen right through the eye's slit. The silhouette of the creature's body cast a shadow somewhere beyond, lost to the shadows of the Deep. As it drew closer, the surface bowed, stretching around the eyeball underneath his hooves. Revelation slapped him in the face. Quickly, his eyes darted above, then to the portal raging behind him, then back to the great eye.

"Light help me, I'm an idiot," he yelped, gripping a whole fistful of chin hair. His feet felt stuck, like they were waiting for his mind to catch up and puzzle all the pieces together.

Tannin's dread of the Narrows. The open hole in the ice, big enough for a fleet . . . the hole. The HOLE! Another piece of the puzzle slammed into place. "By the Silver Cord! It's not a path at all. And it wasn't made by a blasted Summoning

Stone either," he said, still holding the divine Oracle high above his head. "It's *that* thing!" he screeched. "It melted its way through solid ice, and I've been following it the whole time!" He tried willing his legs into submission, to run, or even take a step, but they trembled uncontrollably—his whole body was trembling. *Light of the Dawn, that thing put off some heat,* he thought, shielding his face with his free hand. Steam roiled up from the stygian waters and from his chestnut coat, making it difficult to see. *How could something put off so much heat, in such a cold place?* It seemed impossible, unless the biting chill of the Narrows could somehow refreeze itself around that thing as it tunneled. But even that did not make sense. There was just too much unfrozen water. Mal'ak looked across the black waters. There were no tunnels or paths of ice that he could see. The ice had retreated almost instantly at the beast's approach, and Mal'ak's heart sank as the final piece of the puzzle slammed into place . . . this is where the monster lives.

The Summoning Stone droned out its song. Pale

green energy leaked from the ancient oracle through his fingers, connecting to the portal behind him. He shook all over with that new emotion he had learned and hated most of all: fear—it gripped him like a vice. He willed his legs to move and took a single step.

"By the Lion banner, I *will* move," he said through gritted teeth, taking another.

Steam rose from the boiling sea like hot metal pulled from his forge and plunged into water. It obscured everything, even the portal, but the roar of the portal *was* getting louder and louder, so he moved toward the sound.

"Great Lord, give me strength," he whispered, sliding his way across the dark waters. From the turbid depths, the eye pressed into the surface underneath him, stretching Adam's Ward to the point that Mal'ak feared it would break at any second. He dared not look down, he dared not release the Summoning Stone, and above all else, he dared not stop.

The roar of the portal was deafening.

He was close! Praise the Dawn Bringer, he was close. Biting cold slid over his skin, a cold he could feel even through his coat. But he welcomed the chill this time. The portal slid around him and he even welcomed the fall—*anything* but staying near that thing. *Dawn's Light, anything but the Narrows,* thought Mal'ak.

"Oof!" Falling through the other side of the portal, he met the ground with a thud. Immediately, the portal thinned to a hairline, then winked out, just as before. Mal'ak collapsed in a pile. His legs felt weak, like untempered springs, and his heart was still racing. For the first time since he had left heaven, silence reigned, and Mal'ak sat in it, shivering. No raging portals, no hungry Dragons and, thank the Dawn Bringer, no *Narrows.* Just silence. For the moment, he could think of no better gift than this.

Mal'ak looked toward the horizon. Three-quarters of the earth's moon lit up a black velvet night, back dropped by stars, jewels on display. Sparse trees and clover littered the red lined hills, casting moon-shadows across the clay forest floor. Earth was pretty by moonlight. *This view might be the first pleasant thing that has happened since I got here. Well, that and not landing on my head,* he thought.

Adam's words rang in his ears. *"This will be an adventure never to be forgotten."*

"Adventure?" Mal'ak dry-rung his hands, trying to chase the chill from his bones. "Dawn help me, I can't believe I'm not in the belly of that thing." He tucked the Summoning Stone back inside his pack. It still felt warm sliding within the folds of his tunic. Stretching his legs, he got back to his feet and stood, for a moment, scratching his neck. He breathed in deep, letting his senses roam this new world. This was his second brush with earth time, and by the Dawn Bringer's Light, he would experience it, Dragons or no. There was so much to see here, so much that Adam had *not* told him about earth. The wild smell of soil, the curve of the planet beneath his hooves, even the quirky chirp of a bug's song that filled the cedar and elms of the forest's edge was a wonder. A flicker of movement caught his eye, four deer, grazing on wild clover not far from the forest's edge, one with antlers watching warily from the tree line. By the measurements in Mal'ak's head, he only stood thirty cubits from them, but he could tell they were oblivious. They had no idea that a Ta'ow Crafter was in their forest. He found it strange how the Spirit realm could lay so close to the realm of flesh and yet *apparently* so far. The best Mal'ak could figure, they sat sort of parallel to one another. Like two rooms separated by a one way looking glass. But here on earth, flesh simply did not have the acuity to see it. Out of habit, he fumbled through his pack for his quill and journal, when something gently tugged downward on his limbs. Mal'ak's brow rose. "Gravity!" he said, laughing. "By the Silver Cord. Time!" he gasped. For the second time, Mal'ak felt time. It moved, sliding over, around and between his legs, flowing much like a river, but lighter than water, lighter than air, constant and sure. It was big. No . . . by the Dawn, it was *enormous!* Stars burned the heavens, their planets whirling, spinning upon nothing but invisible currents of gravity, all traveling in perfect synch to measure out the motion defined here as time. And he was inside of it, inside of time just like any Flesh-Walker. It was magnificent. Even fallen as it was, the scope of the Great Lord's gift to man left him speechless. He strained his eyes looking far into the stars, where the wide open spaces of distance raced beyond measuring, beyond reasoning, even beyond him. "It doesn't end," he mumbled. Gazing upward, Mal'ak fell to his knees in open mouthed wonder. He didn't care where he was or what danger might be lurking. The fires of Sheol, Tannin, or the Dragon lord himself could have been standing there, but Mal'ak would not let this moment pass.

"There is glory due," he said resolutely. For the first time in his life, tears welled up in his eyes. He touched the salty liquid slicking his cheeks, and marveled. Tears *never* fell in the Great Lord's Kingdom. He could feel a song rising somewhere deep inside of him, and *nothing* would stop him from offering it. He threw back his head and began to sing:

ANNO DOMINI

Only You, Only You

Beauty upon beauty, Glory upon glory

The only One, the only worthy

Heaven's chambers burst forth with glorious songs

The stars sing of You, they sing of You, my King

Only of You they sing, only You, adoring

The eternal spaces roll out your fame

"The Dawn Bringer comes," is their refrain

And I have joined their song

Due Glory belongs . . . Only You . . . Only You

Beauty upon beauty, Glory upon glory

Only You . . . Only You could do this

CHAPTER 5:
THE HIGH-BOURNE

At the song's last refrain, Mal'ak lowered his eyes from the stars, only to meet the silent stare of an archangel studying him. He had heard nothing, but there he was, silent as a shadow, and more angels appearing by the second. One by one the air quavered, and a new porcelain face unveiled itself. *Have they been here the whole time, cloaked? Dawn's Light, how long had they been watching?* Mal'ak rounded a full circle before coming back to face the angel closest to him. His slender face could have been carved from stone, but somehow managed a softness. Eyes set in ember flame stared at Mal'ak, compassion plain on his face. Not as tall as a Ta'ow, but clearly taller than the others, the angel stood majestic, absolutely regal, with a hawk's brow and penetrating gaze that seemed firmly set within wisdom's own storehouses. *This is not just any High-Bourne*, thought Mal'ak. *This is an archangel. This one is clearly in charge.* Protective Wards cast in Rune-Craft marked his ageless skin, and he carried a quill and oversized book gripped in both hands. The crest of a golden Lion's head was embedded on the cover and seven seals intertwined through the spine of its binding.

"An oracle," Mal'ak muttered.

Before he could say anything else, the angel smiled and said, "We haven't heard a song like that in a very, *very* long time, Ta'ow."

Mal'ak glanced around to see other High-Bourne wiping their eyes, emotion plain on their faces. They all moved with the same sort of sweeping motion that Elisheba had, except the leader, the one directly in front of him.

"My name is Mal'ak—"

CHAPTER 5: THE HIGH-BOURNE

"I know," he said with a smile. "I am the Chronicler, servant of He Who Brings the Dawn, Keeper of the Seven Seals, Keeper of the Ages, and we are the High-Bourne of heaven. Mal'ak of the Ta'ow, there are Dragon about." He did not say it like he was afraid, only that it was a fact. He broke into a bit of a laugh that resonated through the air in multiple frequencies—beautiful, melodic. He glanced toward his tribe, then back to Mal'ak and said, "There are Dragon about, and here you stand, Mal'ak, barely eight furlongs from the front lines . . . singing your song!" There was no condemnation in his words, but something that might have been akin to admiration in the archangel's slender face.

Mal'ak knuckled his neck tentatively. "There was glory due, my Liege," he said, his face heating up.

The Chronicler's eyes gleamed at the corners. "Indeed," he nodded with a smile. "It has begun, then. The General will want to know of your presence. We must make haste."

The next thing Mal'ak knew, four strong hands grabbed him—a set under each arm. He was hoisted skyward, northwest by the looks of it. The rest of the tribe fell into formation around the Chronicler and the two High-Bourne who carried Mal'ak. Once in position, light began to emanate from their wings, white hot, heat rippling the air around them, and then they were gone. Just like that. Mal'ak watched the ground fall away and his escorts disappear one by one. The three remaining High-Bourne flew with Mal'ak in plain view, while the others traveled cloaked and who knew where.

The evening rays of the sun rimmed the mountains to the northwest. Red twilight colored a sliver of moon in a cloudless sky. It was warm and felt good. Mal'ak spread his arms wide, letting the sun warm his bones and time flow through his fingertips, praising the Great Lord's name that he had made it this far. His stomach growled. He felt he could eat his own weight in manna loaf.

"Light, I'm hungry," he said, eyebrows sliding

together . . . Hunger pains—another new sensation he had never experie—

No. Mal'ak pushed it far from his mind. There was no time for such thoughts. The sun was set, all but for pink twilight. It would be dark soon, and he didn't want to think about what might roam the Haze of earth after dark. High above the peaks and dead ahead, the Citadel Ring came into view. It stretched across the upper atmosphere of earth, invisible to humans, but his eyes could easily pick out the network of High-Bourne strongholds far above. It was impressive. A sky fortress that surrounded the entire planet, from what he could see. Its architecture was not as fine as Ta'ow craft, but impressive nonetheless. A cloud city with domes and spires that climbed toward the sun, its sheer faces crafted from a mixture of air and mineral. Light, but extremely strong. Mal'ak had seen this combination of elements before. Minerals provided great strength and air provided the lightness and space for Living Water to circulate within the inner portions of the thick walls.

Simple, but ingenious. A perfect defense against Shadow spawn. From what Mal'ak could tell, the water traveled in a closed circuit, exposed only at great waterfalls that fell from the numerous machicolations situated along the parapets and spire walls. It was beautiful, but deadly. Any demon to actually pierce the thick outer casing of the wall would find a nasty surprise flowing underneath.

They lighted atop a landing on one of the upper spires where a handful of High-Bourne saluted the Chronicler saying, "Honor and strength."

The Chronicler nodded quickly, and kept walking, leading them all into a lofty room, almost as big as the landing they had just lighted upon. It was oval shaped, well lit, with fire Wards floating overhead and around the perimeter. Cornices beveled the walls, adorned in ornate tapestries, embroidered in gold and scarlet silks, skillfully crafted with the unmistakable symbol of the Great Lord emblazoned on the front, a golden Lion. Weapons of war hung from the wall of the round room where not covered in tapestries. Mal'ak's eyes widened. He'd never been in an armory before. Pole-arm and battle-axe followed the wall-line, neatly placed in their casings; ornate shields, scimitar, and broad-swords were propped along holders at the far end of the room, while daggers of all sizes littered the tables and floor, some attached to gauntlets, some free standing, and some were so small, Mal'ak could easily have fit the entire blade into the sleeve of his tunic. But one weapon in particular caught his eye. A war-hammer, propped up on its head, sitting on the floor like it had been forgotten. He could not get a clear look at it, but from what he could make out, it looked massive in scale. That alone would not name its origin, though. It was more than the size. Judging by how perfectly the lines fell along the haft and the unmistakable runes, forge-crafted into the part of the head that he could see from this angle, this weapon was crafted by his Elders. It *was* Ta'ow—he would have bet his horns on it. Fire Wards chased twilight to the fringes of the round room, giving it generous light, but not too much.

The hammer lay beside a plain table in the middle of the room with scrolls and maps strewn on top, with a mountain of an angel crouched over it all. Mal'ak had never seen an angel this large, not of the High-Bourne. At first, he was puzzled by how he had missed the angel's presence, standing right in front of the table like he was, much less an angel of such stature. But the truth of it was that it was hard to set an eye to him, with his wings shifting and bending the light the way all High-Bourne seem to do. It was almost like he was not there at all, but then he was. Of course, the hammer had drawn Mal'ak's eye first. It was a relic from another age. Any Crafter worth his salt would give his best anvil just to study it.

When they reached earshot, the big angel spoke. "But is he the one?"

Mal'ak saw no one else in the round room as the Chronicler replied, "See for yourself, General." As the General turned to face them, the Chronicler deliberated formally: "Mal'ak of the Ta'ow, I give you the General

Archistrategos, Servant of He Who Brings the Dawn, Commander of the High-Bourne tribes, The Great Tacticianer, the very *Tip* of the Sword," he sniffed.

The General rounded on them, and Mal'ak was not quite prepared. *So many names*, he thought. He was already excited about finally meeting the High-Bourne, maybe a little too excited. But the General just about unhinged his nerves. Mal'ak blinked, and suddenly, the General was standing in front of him.

"What is your name, Ta'ow?" Mal'ak's eyes rounded, and his mind might as well have been as blank as a new sheet of journal paper. The General was deep browed and square jawed, with the ageless look of the High-Bourne. Pitch black hair framed his flawless face, falling into the well-muscled crevices of his shoulders as he leaned close to Mal'ak's face. He only wore a feather-cloth tunic that matched the hue of his wings perfectly, gilded in blue runes at the fringes of the arm and neck holes. Wards, if Mal'ak had to guess. Wards and the symbol of the Lion banner emblazoned on the front. His neck and part of his chest had markings as well. But his eyes were what Mal'ak could not escape from. Eyes that could not be met, but could not be ignored. Eyes held in ember flame, the flame of the ages, eyes accustomed to getting an answer. It was a simple question. He didn't yell, but Dawn's Light, if his voice didn't roll like a storm carries thunder.

Mal'ak tried to get something to come out, anything, but it was a struggle just to meet the General's eyes. Light, those eyes could forge metal they burned so hot. Mal'ak had never seen such fierceness. Fear stabbed at his middle . . . He felt a hand on his shoulder and then a cool rush flow into him, calming him, and strength returning to his limbs.

"What did you do to me?" Mal'ak  the Chronicler, still aware of the General's gaze on

"It is called Rune-Craft. I cast a Ward into you. A very small portion of me, spent on you gthen and heal you so . . . ahem, so you can *answer* the General's question."

Chapter 5: The High-Bourne

The General hadn't budged, but waited with an odd look on his face.

"My . . . my name is Mal'ak."

The General leaned in closer, sniffing the air, then exhaled in a puff that blew Mal'ak's fur back. His eyes narrowed. "Where have you been Ta'ow? You reek of Shadow spawn," he said with a taste of disgust.

Mal'ak opened his mouth and everything came pouring out. The Stirring, leaving the Great Lord's Kingdom, his meeting of Elisheba and Tannin. When her name was mentioned, the Chronicler spun him around.

"Where did you last see her?" His face was strained.

"Tannin—" Mal'ak tried to continue but the Chronicler held up his hand as if to say, "Nothing more need be said. The name, Tannin, was enough." His eyes drifted like his mind was somewhere distant.

"She fell," Mal'ak said quietly.

"I should have pulled back," the Chronicler cut in. "*I* should have followed her to the ground, mended her wounds . . . I thought she would be safe, cloaked on the ground . . . so many Legion around, I thought I could distract them from her . . ."

Mal'ak couldn't take it anymore. He bowed down to the Chronicler's feet and clasped them in his hands. "The fault is mine alone," he said. "I landed in the Haze and she protected me. I have never seen such skill with a blade, the way she moved." The General grunted with approval. "I . . . I had to leave her when I entered the Narrows," Mal'ak said, slightly ashamed. "I did not know what else to—"

"Where did you say you were?" the General blurted.

"Oh," Mal'ak said, rustling through his pack. "Light, I almost forgot! I carry a message. It is Sacrosanct," he added, and with that he shoved the Summoning Stone toward them. The General's face froze. He recoiled from the Stone, obviously shocked. He looked at Mal'ak, then he looked at the Stone, then back to Mal'ak again.

"Anathema," whispered the Chronicler. "You faced Tannin, *then* you traversed *through* the Narrows?"

he asked very slowly. Mal'ak's head bobbed up and down anxiously. Mal'ak wasn't sure what Anathema meant, but if the Chronicler's face was any indication, surprise stretched every hard line of that stone facade. "And the Shadow of the Deep?" said the Chronicler. "Did you catch sight of the beast, Leviathan?"

"I saw something there. It was big, and I'm pretty sure it saw me as well," Mal'ak said, his cheeks heating. This brought on a longer silence, and for a moment, downright bafflement on the Chronicler's face.

Suddenly, the General bellowed a laugh that nearly shook the room. He fastened his arms around Mal'ak in a bear hug, hoisting him up in the air.

"Light of the Dawn, little Blacksmith!" he shook with laughter. "You've just arrived and already you surprise me. The fact that you still exist bears proof of your story." Dropping Mal'ak to the floor, he gave him a swat on the back. "Ha! Sacrosanct!" The General apparently approved of his story. Mal'ak was not used to being picked up, or being called "little" for that matter, but figured he would just roll with the General's enthusiasm.

"It *has* begun," the Chronicler spoke as if dazed. "The Epoch Horizon is upon us!"

C HAPTER 6:
THE BREACH

The Epoch Horizon? Mal'ak thought, remembering his words to the gold dragon, Tannin. Words that were not his own.

"What about the Summons?" asked Mal'ak.

"That *is* the Summons," the Chronicler said, pointing to the Summoning Stone in Mal'ak's hand.

"It is?" said Mal'ak, knuckling that marvelous itch just under his bushy chin. "So—if *this* is the Summons, then what is the Epoch Horizon? I don't understand . . ." Mal'ak's voice trailed off, a little embarrassed, but not enough to win out over Ta'ow curiosity.

"The Epoch Horizon is not so much a *what* as it is *in between a when.*"

Mal'ak's brow slumped downward. The Chronicler laughed softly. "Listen and discern," he said, grabbing both of Mal'ak's hands, stretching them outward. "Imagine the Great Lord and his kingdom as a vast wheel. Now imagine that you *are* that wheel . . . that your body is at the center, your elbows are the Narrows and your fingertips are where we are right now . . . earth." He began to turn Mal'ak slowly round and round. "You see? Much like a wheel, the farther you get from the center toward your fingers, the faster the speed.

"So it is with time," the General broke in. "Everything moves with He Who Brings the Dawn, Blacksmith . . . even time."

"Right now we are at His fingertips, here on earth," the Chronicler added with a quick pat to Mal'ak's fingers. "The ragged edges of eternity are all that lie beyond this."

"But what does that have to do with the

80

Summoning Stones?"

"*He* is coming," said the General, stretching out his own arms well beyond Mal'ak's reach. "You see, The Dawn Bringer transcends time, so we have been *Summoned* to a place *in between* time, to witness his coming *into* time."

"*The Epoch Horizon . . .*" The words spilled from Mal'ak's mouth as understanding took a hold. "*He* is coming?"

"Precisely." The Chronicler nodded with satisfaction. "And the only place out of phase with time . . ."

"The Narrows!" Mal'ak butted in, his stomach suddenly knotting up again.

"Well done, Blacksmith," the General said, swatting him on the back so hard Mal'ak almost fell over.

"You will train as we go. The Chronicler will instruct you in the fine art of Rune-Crafting, and I will see to your combat. We will spare you no quarter, Mal'ak of the Ta'ow. I will teach you the Precepts of War just like I have to my High-Bourne. You will learn to follow orders like a High-Bourne, to fight like a High-Bourne. You will learn what it means to *be* High-Bourne, or you will die. And if you die—you will die like a High-Bourne." The General's eyes flashed, both hands balling into a fisted salute:"*My life for yours, your life for mine. Honor and Strength . . . for the KING!* Say it!"

Mal'ak swallowed hard, twice, trying to work some moisture back into his mouth. *What are the Precepts of War?* thought Mal'ak. The hair on the back of his neck bristled. He met the General's flame golden eyes but didn't flinch this time. Balling his own hands into fists, he snapped them across his chest and swore by the Lion banner:

"All that I am is yours. *My Life for yours, your life for mine. Honor and Strength . . . for the KING!*

The General grunted in approval. "Welcome to the High-Bourne. We will go when the sun reaches the solstice."

Suddenly, the door swung open from the other end of the room and a broad-nosed High-Bourne stepped inside. He was tall, with a square jaw and stately grace, similar to the Chronicler in a manner, but somehow less.

CHAPTER 6: THE BREACH

"My apologies, my lieges," he said, giving a studied nod to Mal'ak. "There has been a breach!

"Where, Tachan?" the General barked.

"The Bullwarks, my General. There is Legion within the Citadel!" The angel known as Tachan wore that ageless mask of serenity that seemed more cut from stone than anything living, but the wild in his eyes told another tale.

Mal'ak heard a rumble from the General that chilled his bones. The next thing he knew, he was being lifted off of the ground like he weighed nothing. It all happened so fast he wasn't sure if it was the General or the Chronicler who grabbed him. When his senses caught up, the corridors of the Citadel Ring were rushing by in a blur. Through passages and doors they flew. Suddenly, they were outside in the open air. Mal'ak recognized the same walls they had flown over on his flight in with the Chronicler. *The Bullwarks*, he thought. Dawn's Light! He was flying with High-Bourne—into *battle*, nonetheless! He heard a voice in his head.

'Whatever happens, stay close to me. And if it is

83

not sworn to the Lion banner . . . kill it!'

Mal'ak looked up. It was the General carrying him in one hand, in the other he carried the long handled hammer. From this close, Mal'ak could tell it was carved from Storm Crystal. There was a familiar contour to the hammer's lines. *Perfect* symmetry. That alone told him it was Ta'ow crafted, and any doubts he had before, however small, were completely gone now. He smiled, satisfied. It was ancient; maybe forged in the Age of the Turning, maybe even before. He felt the ground under his hooves again. The world stopped whooshing by and his mouth gaped. Within the inner wall of the Bullwarks was a hole. No more than two cubits wide and as tall. The top of a demon's head had broken clean through to the inside.

"Anathema! A Kolossos!" the Chronicler said, pointing at a bald, high cheeked demon with a pinched face and fat nose staring glassy-eyed back at them.

CHAPTER 6: THE BREACH

Mal'ak could not see the rest of the demon's body, but judging by the size of its head, plugging up the hole in the wall, it was big—really big. Two large, slate colored horns, longer than Mal'ak's own, extruded from the top of its head. Its mouth stretched wide open, while out of it, crawled a clutch of something small and fast.

"Trogs!" growled the General, as he watched the rat sized abominations push their way past the fat lips of the Kolossos and into the room. Small and spindly, they spread across the floor like poured liquid. Their speed made it all but impossible for Mal'ak to distinguish anything other than short red horns and talons. The rest was a blur.

Mal'ak could not believe how many burrowed up from inside the belly of the beast. The Bullwarks' defenses held true, though. Living water gushed freely from the breach down onto the Kolossos's head. It spasmed, hair and scales falling off in clumps. The left side of its face was partially melted away, but it kept its mouth open in that silent scream, its head protecting the smaller legion of demons clawing their way up from inside its belly.

CHAPTER 7:
SHAMAYIN

The Chronicler disappeared without a word. The General crouched low, spreading his wings like a bird of prey, each feather glowing white hot around the edges, like bladed embers drawn from the fires of Mal'ak's kiln back home. Mal'ak took a step back. It all was happening so fast, too fast. Numbers fell across everything in a jumble, rate of speed, overlapping distance, and other measurements his mind just threw into the mix for good measure. Trogs poured from the Kolossos's mouth in mind numbing quantities. The floor was covered with the little beasts.

'The hammer, Shamayin,' the General's voice broke inside his head. 'Pick it up Blacksmith! Let us see you wield a weapon of the Elders.'

Glancing down, the hammer lay at Mal'ak's feet. He did not remember it having a name, or remember seeing the General put it there, but it was there now. Mal'ak grasped one end of the long hammer. Now if he could just stop his hands from shaking. Suddenly, the wooden haft of the ancient weapon grew right through his fingers. Snaking up, it grabbed his right forearm, forming wooded plates from his elbow up to his shoulder.

"It's got me!" Mal'ak yelped. "Dawn's Light, get it off!" He flailed around the room, pulling at it, shaking the ancient hammer wildly, but it wouldn't budge. "Someone get it off!" he yelled, staggering into the General, almost knocking him over.

Smash! Smash! Desperate, he tried slamming it against the floor of the Bullwarks to dislodge it. Smash! Stress cracks spider webbed across the floor between his legs. The General ducked as a crushing blow thundered into the wall inches from his head.

"Sheol's flames, Blacksmith!" the General burst out. "Who are you trying to hit? Us or them?"

"Focus, Mal'ak." The Chronicler's voice was crystal chimes that cut through the chaos in Mal'ak's head. "The hammer is attuned to what you *most* need. It will release you when it is time to be released."

Mal'ak felt an invisible hand touch his shoulder and a cool weave of spirit flow into him again. Calm, and the cold snap of strength coursed through him just as he remembered earlier. His chest began to rise and fall more slowly. "Steady," he told himself, feeling his heart slow. He focused his thoughts on the hammer's smooth wood haft grown around the contours of his hand. It fit perfectly, with just enough range of motion around his hand to wiggle his thick fingers. It felt good in his hands. It felt—Ta'ow.

"Your training begins now!" the General bellowed. "Swing."

Mal'ak entered back into the moment with a wide

arcing swing of the hammer, but touched nothing. He swung again, and again—all misses. The fallen Legion skittered across the floor like flat stones dancing across water. War felt so different than he'd imagined, more alien than he'd ever dreamed. It had a scent, acrid, vivid. A scent forged in fear and rage. The General was definitely the latter. He could have been a living blade. He moved, no, he sliced through the room, stance after stance in a rhythm so natural, it felt as if he were at dance with himself, but *this* dance was lethal.

'Patience of the mountain,' came the General's voice inside Mal'ak's head as the General's own head swiveled around, then leveled. "Face of the wind," he whispered, fanning his wings, flowing into the next stance. "Conquer like the Flame." In a blur, his wings flexed, slice, slice, slice. Demon parts fell to the ground, essence splattered across the walls and Mal'ak's face. Mal'ak blinked, wiping essence out of his eyes as the General spun into a low crouch. Every step had purpose, efficient, deadly. His movements were reminiscent of Elisheba's cat-like grace, but more powerful in execution, a lion to her lynx. Mal'ak felt clumsy and slow.

"Swing where they *will* be, Blacksmith, not where there are," the General bellowed, carving another swath through the air.

The Precepts of War, thought Mal'ak. *He made* Conquer like the Flame *look easy.* "They're too small," Mal'ak shouted, biting his lip. *Too many lines. Too many numbers.* He was panicking. Fear stabbed at his gut, threatening to freeze his legs again. *If I could just sort out the numbers*, he thought. *So many . . . Wait! The numbers!*

Swing where they will be—not where they are! Mal'ak scanned the floor again. He let his peripheral vision take in *all* of the room, not just what was in front of him. If his hunch was right, he might not have to swing faster, just smarter. The numbers and lines in his head fell differently on buildings and weapons than on the living, but as a Crafter he could track the lines of most any measurement. Mal'ak's mouth fixed in a hard line. Linear measurements were useless at this point. The filthy little beasts would be long gone before his hammer could strike home. So he began tracking averages—distance in relation to speed and elevation. Somewhere between the milliseconds, an anomaly formed. The lines were still there, as always, the measurements intact, but probability itself seemed to manifest a pattern over them, over the numbers. "Is that the Quintessence?" Mal'ak gasped, as transparent spirals formed around each demon in a pattern, and larger spirals formed around groups that moved as a swarm. It was faint, like the image of an image, but there it was. Mal'ak grinned.

"The Quintessence," he said. "By the Dawn! It manifests in patterns of probability." Gritting his teeth, he swung the ancient hammer along the surface of the patterned spiral. Wham! Demon essence splattered the walls.

The General was positioned firmly to the right of the cramped room so it was easy to know which direction they would jump first. One look at him and they *all* jumped as far left as they could. From there the numbers did the rest. The tide was turning quickly. The Chronicler appeared toward the back of the room—it was the only way in or out. His voice droned softly in a rhythmic chant.

Dawn's Light, it sounded like the Old Tongue to Mal'ak. But no one had uttered those Canticles since the Age of the Turning. He wanted to hear more, but concentration would not allow it. Demons poured from the Kolossos's mouth faster than he could swing. Suddenly, living water flowed from the fisher in the wall off of the Kolossos's half melted head toward the Chronicler. The clear liquid heaped up onto itself until it formed a wall of living water in the doorway.

"He's commanding the water?" Mal'ak blurted, half laughing out loud. "Look General, he's commanding the wa—."

"Concentrate," the General snapped, narrowly snatching a Trog, barely an arm's length from Mal'ak's throat. It squealed when the General twisted it in two halves with his bare hands. He flicked the mangled body to the ground like a rag, terror frozen in its dead eyes. The acrid stench of the Kolossos's cooking head hung thick in the air, mixed with the metallic odor of demon insides that stirred Mal'ak's stomach. With the door sealed up by a wall of living water, the Chronicler had turned his attention to the Kolossos now. Its head looked the size of a good anvil, and probably as hard. In fact, Mal'ak realized the Legion had made use of its head as a battering ram to penetrate the wall. It had not survived the impact, but served its purpose nonetheless. Its mouth was stretched wide by Shadow-Bind, dark magic, forcing the dead demons mouth open far too wide to be normal. The Chronicler's rhythmic chant flowed through the air, rising and falling. The water obeyed, like it *wanted* to do his bidding—like it had been waiting on the Chronicler to ask. Living liquid continued to flow out of the wall, accumulating around the melting head of the Kolossos in a boiling ball. Deftly, it made its way down the Kolossos's throat. Muted squeals reached all the way through the stomach lining of the big demon's insides.

"Mal'ak!" yelled the General, as searing pain slid into Mal'ak's back. Something was on his back, positioned so he could not reach it. He could see just enough of the spindly little beast to make out small red horns, black taloned hands and feet, and a circular mouth lined with rows of teeth. Pain surged up his spine. Another first. Pain. The little demon twisted its razored fingers deeper and began to bite. Mal'ak roared. Patches of yellow flashed in his eyes. Pain and something else rose within him, coming alongside the panic. He couldn't reach the filthy little demon and realized that if he didn't do something, it would quite literally eat its way inside him.

'Hold still!' came the General's voice in his head, but the voice seemed distant now. All Mal'ak could see was red. The red rage of battle. It swallowed his pain and his fear whole. His hands balled into fists, he lowered his head, and charged for the nearest wall. *Boom! Boom! Boom!* Each impact had the effect of an earthquake, shaking the entire room as he slammed his back against it. The fortified walls of the Bullwarks shook with the impact. Finally, he felt the beast loosen its grip and fall to the floor. Mal'ak spun on his heal, tracking the lines of probability. He swung the ancient hammer in a semi-circle across the surface of the sphere. *Smash! Smash! Smash!*

"It is dead, Mal'ak."Smash!"Mal'ak! They're *all* dead," said the Chronicler.

Mal'ak's chest heaved. He felt a hand on his shoulder and a cool weave of spirit soothe the pounding of his heart. Slowly, it steadied to an even rhythm. The red in his eyes faded and the hammer suddenly released him.

"Ahem . . . That is one way to do it," the Chronicler said with a sniff, taking the hammer from Mal'ak, haft first. Mal'ak hadn't noticed that in the melee of things, he had been holding the ancient weapon upside down, by its head. His cheeks felt warm all of the sudden.

"By the Silver Cord, Blacksmith. You might have brought the entire Bullwarks down on us had you held it proper." The General looked around with a grin.

Mal'ak's cheeks flushed the shade of three sunsets. "I'm sorry," he said.

"Sorry?" the Chronicler mused. "The art of war is

drawn in the blood of experience—our own experiences, Mal'ak. Unfortunately, there is no other canvas. You are alive, the Dawn shine its light upon us, and today, that is good enough." He smiled, glancing down at the hammer.

It looked big in his hands, at least, to Mal'ak it did. Of course, if he was right, it was forged by the Elder Ta'ow. His Elders were as big as he was—some even larger.

"You will need Ward-Crafting to tend to the wound on your back, and plenty of rest—the *real* kind," said the Chronicler, holding the hammer eye level, and looking down its shaft approvingly. "A finer weapon, I've not seen in the realms, save one."

"Aye." The General nodded.

They both looked around the room, the General cleaning his wings, the Chronicler shaking his head at the mess they had made while fingering the runes on the ancient hammer, and both of them suddenly talking like they had just sat down for dinner. Mal'ak noticed that archangels had a knack for doing that sort of thing. Nerves of steel and a peculiar gifting of concurrent thought. This was something a bit beyond Ta'ow abilities, but they seemed well adapted to it. Mal'ak generally liked to take one thought at a time. That was the Ta'ow way. Adam's stories had helped prepare him for this sort of thing, to a certain degree, but it was quite different to actually watch them do it.

The Chronicler and the General stood ankle deep in demon remains, engaged in thought and conversation about the old hammer, and yet Mal'ak could tell they were both somewhere else entirely in their heads. Sometimes it seemed as if their bodies were completely independent of their minds altogether. He had watched them work with their hands while looking at something else, while having a conversation totally unrelated to either. It was quite disconcerting, but fascinating to watch. He would have to record this in his journal for later study.

The Chronicler still caressed the haft of the old hammer thoughtfully. After a moment, a soft glow radiated under his fingers from the head of the ancient weapon. This seemed to draw his full attention. The head was a single piece—perfectly carved from Storm Crystal, found only near the Great Lord's throne and nowhere else. It was gilded with an overlay of Silver Weave cast in the shape of runes that were forged right onto the stone itself. Only Forge-Craft could shape a weapon like this. And only a Crafter could Forge-Craft. Mal'ak's chest swelled. That the Elder Ta'ow could have forged such a formidable weapon filled him with remarkable delight. The lines fell along the face of the hammer perfectly, no matter what angle you looked from, but the haft was what fascinated Mal'ak the most. As if reading his thoughts, the Chronicler held it up, eye level.

"You see there?" he asked, pointing to the wooden shaft. Mal'ak squinted. He could barely make out the faint shift in grain pattern at the halfway point.

"It has been grafted—forged of two halves. Crafters." He chuckled under his breath. "I do not know how they accomplished this, but in the Third Age, at Eden's end, your Elders somehow grafted together two branches from *two* separate Aspects."

Mal'ak's mouth fell open. "You mean these were cut from—"

"One from the Tree of Knowledge of Good and Evil. The other, from the Tree of Life itself." The Chronicler smiled at Mal'ak's unusual quiet. Highly unusual for a Ta'ow.

"It held onto me . . ." Mal'ak mumbled.

"Yes, and it will do more than that. Weapons like these, the *best* weapons, attune themselves to only one," the Chronicler said with a tone of respect. "I have never seen its like, and I have never seen it quicken to another's touch either. Perhaps it is because you are Ta'ow. Perhaps it sees more in you than you see in yourself. Either way, this weapon has chosen who will wield it. Keep it safe and it will keep you safe." And with that, the Chronicler held the ancient hammer out to Mal'ak.

Mal'ak reached uneasily for the hammers haft. *The right end this time,* he thought.

CHAPTER 7: SHAMAYIN

"Leviathan's beard, Blacksmith, just take it," the General said, with an approving grin.

"This was a red herring." The Chronicler rounded on the General. His tone was serious now, almost like another thought pattern had interrupted the previous. "We have already lost precious moments, and now even more, thanks to the Kolossos."

"Tannin," the General said the name through gritted teeth.

"How long *were* you in the Narrows?" the General asked, looking more concerned than Mal'ak would have liked.

"I'm not sure," Mal'ak said, rubbing his neck. "Everything was white ice and black water. I'm not used to how time moves and—"

"No matter," the Chronicler cut in. "Time moves differently there anyway. It could have been a day, maybe two. The Dawn forbid it was any more than that. Tannin has the other Summoning Stone, and I'm sure his masters

103

will use it accordingly.

"Are the Stryders sea worthy, General?"

"Of course they are." The General's voice sounded confident but his face bore lines of concern.

"I know you, and I know that look," said the Chronicler. "Your thoughts already reach far ahead of us now, but I would know of your solicitude with the Stryders."

"Aye." The General let out a sigh. "There is no craft more seaworthy than the Stryders, " he said flatly. "It was *their* steady bearing that brought us to this world's shores. It's just—" He pursed his lips, and looked the Chronicler dead in the eye. "Intelligent they may be, Gabriel, *and* swift, but they were never meant for the rigors of war. They are sleek and fast, but their bodies are weakest along the figurehead. If I were Legion, I would . . ." He cut off his words shaking his head as if he did not want to go there mentally.

"I see no other options," said the Chronicler.

"Aye." The General nodded. "Time will not allow us another option. It is settled then. We will protect the

CHAPTER 7: SHAMAYIN

Stryders as best we can, and pray the Dawn shines its favor upon us. We leave at the Solstice."

CHAPTER 8: THE PRECEPTS OF WAR

The Narrows spread out before Mal'ak, an endless black sea of water and ice. It was not as one dimensional as he'd first thought. Land lay far to the north—mountains, several thousand cubits high by the looks of it. It was hard to tell, with their peaks hidden in the mist. Home to the Daq, the small peoples of the north. At least, that is what the High-Bourne had told him. One sentry said that the Daq were a lot like Crafters, gifted in the art of Forge-Crafting. He wanted very much to meet a Daq, but was doubtful it would ever happen. He'd already traveled these forsaken lands once, for what must have been days, and never seen hide nor hair of another living soul besides the monster that resided in these waters. Apparently, there *was* more to this place than he had imagined, though. The Chronicler called it the realm of the Aspects. It was beautiful—in its own way. A black sea reflecting the pale glow of the horizon gave the stygian waters a mirrored finish that looked solid enough to walk on, even without his cloak. But Mal'ak knew better. And the view from his perch was nothing short of magnificent. He stood with the wind pelting his coat atop the sleek wooded bow of a Sea Stryder. Across the dark waters, the Stryders numbered in the billions, enough for every angel, enough for all of heaven's host. To Mal'ak, each enchanted vessel was a majestic symbol to the wonder of this place. Like something born of the sea, they sliced their way through the black and brine, navigating the waters as effortless as trout in a stream. The sleek contour of their bodies perfectly fitted the task of sailing these harsh seas—if you wanted to call it sailing. They actually swam.

CHAPTER 8: THE PRECEPTS OF WAR

Mal'ak loved enchanted wood. He watched, fascinated, as the Stryder's tail gently flexed, cresting the surface, then thrusting downward, leaving a perfect foamy swirl in its wake. It served as both rudder and propulsion. *Marvelous*, he thought, smiling. *Now* this *is the way to travel the Narrows. Adam would never believe this.* Mal'ak's smile suddenly thinned as he glanced northeast of their bearing.

Dark soot lengthened the skyline, the telltale signs that the Dreadnought fleet of the Legion had passed through these waters. They dotted the horizon, some not too far ahead. At least the rear of the fleet was in plain view. Giant black engines on a black sea—no mast or sail. All steam, and whirring gears, plowing a smoky path of foam in the abyssal depths. By the lines, their four red stacks stood four to five times higher than any Stryder, with green flames belching from the holes. The decks were lined with all manner and rank of demon. The sides were plated with metal forged from something that Mal'ak either couldn't recognize from this distance or from metallurgy that he'd never seen before. *Curious . . . very curious,* he thought. He was also curious as to what was powering the Dread engines. He had asked earlier, but the Chronicler just looked at him in that knowing stare and said, "There is knowledge that is too great, dear Mal'ak, secrets hidden that are better left that way." Then he walked away, just like that. Whatever was powering those monstrosities could not be good.

The day stretched on here, just like he remembered, unchanging twilight, with a chill that bit deeper as they went. His training had continued nonstop for five days now. At least, that was the estimated time by the General. Mal'ak was sick of training, sick of Precepts, and frankly, plain old exhausted. His ears drooped as the General barked out another Precept.

"*Consume Like the Flame*, Mal'ak! Push!"

"I am," grunted Mal'ak, his fingers interlocking with the General's.

"No, you are not," the General said with a sharp snort. "Precept Four is *Consume Like the Flame*, not *Bend like the Forest*.

Chapter 8: The Precepts of War

You can feign weakness somewhere else. You are no longer in heaven and you are *certainly* not weak. I have told you, I will spare you no quarter, and neither will they." Little effort registered in the General's eyes. The hard angles of his ageless face stood motionless against the rushing wind crossing the wooded prow of the Sea Stryder's deck. "To be Ta'ow is to be strong. *Be strong,*" he said, with a sliver of frustration.

Mal'ak was listening—really he was. When the General spoke, everyone did. He wanted to *Consume Like the Flame,* but his thoughts were, well, split. His mind drifted toward her without even realizing it. *Is she okay? What is Tannin doing to her? Elisheba . . . If only I hadn't left her. If only I could have—*

The General swatted his hands away. Swatted them away like they were nothing. A viselike grip clamped onto Mal'ak's horns. The metallic scrape of High-Bourne skin sliding against his horns made the hair on his ears stand straight up. His face met the General's knee with such force that his vision tunneled and he nearly blacked out.

"What are you doing?" Mal'ak yelped, grabbing his muzzle. A blow to the back of his legs almost buckled his knees. Another across the back of his head made him see yellow splotches. "I don't understand," he said, his voice shaking. Mal'ak could hear fear creeping up again.

"Get up, Blacksmith." The General's voice was more growl than words. Mal'ak wobbled to his feet. Eyes set in ember flame, framed in the wisdom of the ages, measured him. The kind of eyes that give hell-spawn nightmares.

"I'm only going to say this once," the General managed through clenched teeth. "You could never have saved her, Blacksmith. She is Elisheba, High-Bourne, servant of He Who Brings the Dawn, Protector of the Seven Seals, and heir to the Chronicler himself." He said her titles with obvious veneration.

"She was never *yours* to save." Another blow to the stomach doubled Mal'ak over, and his knees thudded to the wooded prow.

"It was her job to save you, Ta'ow. Her road is now

112

marked with a suffering you could not imagine. But she is High-Bourne. She will serve the Great Lord even there—*especially* there. She will earn a new name before her path is done."

Wham! Mal'ak arched his back trying to get away from the pain, but his legs were numbing.

Earn a new name? thought Mal'ak. He had no idea what the General was talking about. High-Bourne ways were strange sometimes, and at the moment he didn't care about new names or High-Bourne ways. Besides, his face hurt too bad to ask. By the Silver Cord, it hurt too much to even think at the moment.

"Please!" Mal'ak whimpered.

Wham! Wham! "Do not feel sorry for her, Blacksmith. Her offering to the Great Lord will now be priceless." The General's voice never changed, but the yellow splotches in Mal'ak's vision morphed into scarlet.

"As far as Dragons are concerned," the flame in the General's eyes flared hotter from the corners. "Dragons are beyond you yet. I will contend with Tannin. Now—I have given you this knowledge as a gift. Rest in it. But so help me, Blacksmith—" Wham! "If you do not concentrate on your training—" Wham! "If you diminish her sacrifice by not giving completely all that you are in this training—" Wham! "I will save Tannin the trouble and beat you until there is nothing left, before I let you put any more of my High-Bourne at risk."

Mal'ak's heart was pumping so loud in his head, he barely heard the last phrase. Rage, the red rage of war numbed him to fear, numbed him to pain. He roared, lowered his head and charged. The bow of the Stryder flexed underneath his hooves as he pushed forward. His horns struck the General flush in the torso, sending out shockwaves that boomed across the Narrows. The General grunted.

"By the Silver Cord! What have I . . . what have I done?" Mal'ak's ears wilted. "What in Heaven's Light was I thinking? I just . . . I just made you grunt and—"

"The favor of the Dawn Bringer shine on you both,"

rumbled a voice like the bending groan of a forest oak. Onyia of the Sea Stryders bent her long neck around to greet them. "My General," she spoke slow and deliberate, her voice pluming the cold air with mist from a mouth as wide as one of Mal'ak's furnaces back home.

"If you continue your training," she said, "I fear this young Ta'ow may crack my hull like an egg." Onyia's face was mild and caring, and as smooth as wood would permit.

"Apologies, Onyia," the General said with a slight bow. "His training is extreme, but of a necessity. However, I would not have your hull pay the cost. I have been searching for his strength for five days now and—"

"And as providence would have, I believe you have found it," the Chronicler's songlike voice broke in.

"Aye." The General nodded, a slight curve touching his lips.

"Wait, I . . . I was a-afraid," Mal'ak said, his ears quivering in a droop. "I mean . . . you wouldn't stop hitting me, and there was this red . . . just, well . . . red! Then I hit you back and . . . and, by the Dawn, I hit you! Please forgive me. I should never have—"

"Forgive you? I was beginning to wonder how long you were going to let me beat on you, Blacksmith," the General said with a shake of his head.

"You mean . . . it was a test?" Mal'ak ears wilted all the way to his cheeks. He knuckled his neck again. It was sore. Of course, his whole body ached. How the General could beat him so badly and not spill a drop of essence was nothing short of astonishing. *Not even a bloodied nose,* he thought wryly. "Are all High-Bourne trained like this?" Mal'ak asked.

"No, they are not. And *this* is not merely a training session in combat." The Chronicler paused, his face drawn with concern. "*This* is me and your General trying to keep you alive. For the extreme measures used, you have at least *my* sympathies." The Chronicler sniffed curtly, with a raised brow angled toward the General, who snorted with a shrug. "Painful as it seems, I *can* heal you. But the General is right.

116

CHAPTER 8: THE PRECEPTS OF WAR

This is nothing to what you will face out there, and it is the quickest way to your strength—your gifting. You will need all of it, Mal'ak. All of your strength, and all of your other gifts if you are to survive your Calling."

"I have other giftings?" Mal'ak queried, his eyes perking up just a bit.

"Haste is paramount, *paramount*," the Chronicler continued as if Mal'ak hadn't spoken. "Our time is borrowed at best. Even this conversation is a gross indulgence in what we simply do not have. Now please, you must be attentive."

The General took over without a pause. "The red you saw was your anger. Anger itself is not wrong so long as it is guided by wisdom. Here in the Narrows and on earth, there is a time for anger. It is actually the proper response to injustice. Here and on earth you must learn to temper your anger with wisdom, for it is with wisdom that we will harness your anger and focus that great strength of yours. Then with *courage* . . ." a savage gleam sparked in the General's golden eyes. "With *courage* we'll unleash that

117

strength of yours upon our enemies and crush the Legion all the way back to the pit."

Mal'ak nodded, knuckling his neck again.

"Why are you pawing at your neck?" The Chronicler's eyes flickered toward the General almost too fast for him to notice—almost. "Are you injured from your training? Are you ill?"

Mal'ak hurt from the top of his fur all the way down to bottom of his hooves. If he told the truth, there really wasn't much left on him that wasn't aching, throbbing, or burning.

"Well, my throat itches just a little," he said, uncertainly.

The Chronicler and the General moved toward him in unison.

"Oh, Dawn's Light," he said, his ears drooping to his cheeks again. "What is it? What have I done now?" He took a step back. "If this is another test, please . . . I mean no disrespect. I'm just now feeling the back of my legs again."

"Did you lose consciousness at any point while captive?" the Chronicler spoke in a buzz, almost too fast to understand.

CHAPTER 8: THE PRECEPTS OF WAR

So that's who Elisheba learned that from, Mal'ak thought.

"Answer him, Blacksmith!" the General barked.

"Well . . . yes, I suppose. I do remember waking up somewhere dark." Mal'ak pawed at his neck again, trying a different tactic to maybe ease the tension. "Have you ever *tried* scratching an itch? I think it feels wonderful. Adam said that humans do it all the ti—"

"Tannin!" The name emptied from both of the High-Bourne's mouths at the same time.

In the next breath, the General was on top of him. *Tackled* him, was more like it.

"Dawn's Light!" Mal'ak screeched.

"Hold him!"

"Aye," the General said, holding Mal'ak firmly, encircling him in his arms and legs.

"I—I'm sorry," Mal'ak said, too exhausted to fight back. "I won't scratch it again. I promise."

The Chronicler grabbed his mouth and pried it open as Halo's light glimmered just above their heads. Mal'ak watched, horrified, as a focused beam of light shot straight down into his throat. By the expression on the Chronicler's face, this was *not* part of his training.

A reflection appeared above him. The Chronicler was spinning weaves of light from Halo and air that somehow mirrored an image of them both. He could see himself now. He could see down his own throat, and in the darkness— something was looking back at him. Small black eyes that alluded to an intelligence peered up from inside of him.

"Anathema! A Wyrm," the Chronicler said, breathless.

Mal'ak's eyes grew three sizes. He realized the mirror image was not for him to see, but for the General to see and confirm. His body spasmed with panic.

"Hold him," the Chronicler shouted. Mal'ak felt the General stiffen. He might as well have been thrashing against Storm Crystal. Arms squeezed around his ribs like bronze coils. Mal'ak thought he might burst like a grape.

"You *will* calm yourself," the Chronicler said, flat eyed. "If you do not, it will hull your brain out like a melon

and you *will* die."

Mal'ak bobbed an open mouthed nod and tried to swallow his heart back down into his chest.

"Now, you have a Wyrm inside of you, a half-life in your neck," the Chronicler said.

"Sheol's flames," the General growled. "That damnation in his gullet has been eavesdropping on us the whole time. That is the only reason he is not in a Dragon's belly right now. We are compromised!"

"Caannin?" Mal'ak asked, his mouth still full of the Chronicler's fingers.

"No, not Tannin... *Lucifer*," the Chronicler corrected him. "Please now, hold still. The nature of this creature's power is rooted in the dominion of the Maleficus Tome. It resists me—"

"By the Silver Cord!" The General glared. "You forget yourself, Gabriel."

The Chronicler never raised his eyes but simply replied, "He deserves to know what is trying to kill him. He deserves the truth, and I would share with him as much of it as I can spare. Truth we have in abundance, dear General. *Time* however . . ." His words trailed off to a whisper.

The General snorted his disapproval.

"The Icamuus?" Mal'ak tried to say.

"Yes, yes, the *Tome of Maleficus*. It is a book."

"EEre's a ook in my eeck?"

"No," the Chronicler rolled his eyes. "The creature draws power and life from a book. Lucifer's book. Now stop talking. The Wyrm is only a larva, but it knows what we're up to."

"Can you reach it?" the General asked.

"The Dawn favor us, yes. They must have triggered it prematurely. I suppose they had to. Right now it is eating its way out of a chrysalis. I cannot cut through it without killing Mal'ak in the process. When the larva frees itself, I will snare it with a weave of air before it has the chance to burrow."

"Aye. It knows what we're up to, larva or no and so does the Legion now. Because it hears, they hear. I should've

122

seen this coming, singe them all! I should have seen this coming. One bite, one drop of Mal'ak's essence spilled, and the Shadow of the Deep will come for us all."

Mal'ak wasn't sure the Chronicler heard a word the General had said. By his expression, he might as well have been listening to him talk about the weather, or how perfectly Onyia's side fins and tail were attuned to cutting through water. His porcelain face was hard lipped concentration, yet blank as slate around his eyes.

"Do you have it?" the General asked again.

Suddenly, the Chronicler's breath caught. His hands clenched, wrenching the sides of Mal'ak's mouth. Stunned resignation raised his eyes to Mal'ak's and he whispered a breathless, "No."

Mal'ak doubled over. His chest burned like open flame had been pressed to it.

"It is burrowing," the Chronicler yelled.

In one motion, the General released Mal'ak and was by his side. Mal'ak could taste the metallic tang of essence leaking onto his tongue.

"Keep your mouth closed, Blacksmith. I know it hurts, but whatever you do, don't open it." Boom! The Narrows began to boil like a cauldron.

"He is near," Onyia shouted, as she crested a wave twenty cubits high.

"You are not dying on me this day. Do you hear me, Blacksmith? How much longer does he have?"

"The Wyrm is tied to the Maleficus Tome, its dominion is of the fallen world, of earth. That is why it resists me. It is bound to him by his own fears. I have done all I can. It is up to him now."

"*Fear.*" The General pronounced the word like he had the Blight itself in his mouth.

The sound of timber cracking rang through the air. Onyia shrieked. Mal'ak looked up in time to see part of her bow and a portion of her face fall away into the murk of the Narrows . . . gone—just gone! The sound of death echoed on the wind and across the waters. Sea Stryders were dodging, diving, anything to escape. All of a sudden, Onyia beached upon something. Her bow pitched upwards a full twenty degrees by Mal'ak's eye.

"He is underneath us," she yelled as they all slid toward the aft. Mal'ak felt someone grab a handful of fur on his back. Power filled him to the brim as he slid, an icy torrent of cold that blasted through his limbs. It jump started his senses, overcame the stabbing ache inside of him; it transcended everything. It even seemed to slow the Wyrm burrowing in his chest. Slamming into the aft railing, they jolted to a stop. Mal'ak whirled around to see the Chronicler's hand fall limply from his back. A songlike murmur fell from the archangel's mouth as he closed his eyes. *"My life for yours, your life for mine. Honor and Strength . . . for the KING!"*

Suddenly the General's voice was in Mal'ak's head. *'Is your calling Sacrosanct?'*

Tears streamed down Mal'ak's face, soaking into his muzzle.

'*Is your calling Sacrosanct?* Answer me!' The voice boomed across their mind link. Mal'ak nodded. '*THEN YOU CANNOT FAIL. DO YOU HEAR ME BLACKSMITH? We are High-Bourne, Shade of His Hand. Let courage rise, Blacksmith. Let courage rise up. Slay this fear with your Calling.*'

From out of nowhere, Shamayin was in his hands. Mal'ak gripped the ancient hammer in both hands. He could feel the direction of the grain in the wooded haft, smooth and even. He could feel the almost imperceptible seam that linked the two ancient Aspects together into one. He could feel . . . everything. The creature stirred slowly in his chest. He knew what he must do. In truth, it seemed obvious now.

Mal'ak leaped to his feet. Power surged through his core—it seemed to be leaking out of every hair on his coat. The Chronicler's power. "I had no idea." He gulped in astonishment. The runes warded into the cowl of his cloak glowed a soft blue. His tongue rolled in his mouth, half full with the metallic taste of his own essence. He clamped his lips, gripped Shamayin, and leaped overboard into the

Deep. His feet puckered the surface of the black liquid, but remained aloft just as before. Adam's Ward on his cloak held fast. He felt light and strong... *very* strong. He leaped forty spans above an oncoming wave that crashed into Onyia, and set out toward the Legion with all his might. Onyia moaned, but Mal'ak didn't look back. His eyes narrowed on the horizon. The Legion held a bearing northeast of him, four thousand and three hundred cubits at twenty-four knots, by the numbers in his head. At current pace, he could overcome them in exactly thirty-five seconds. He would accelerate by 3.2309847 percent and overtake them in seventeen.

Light of the Dawn, his feet were warm. A shadow swelled behind him, a black shade in the stygian sea. Mal'ak felt the wake of the beast swell the water beneath his feet, but didn't stop running—couldn't stop running, not now. Especially now. He didn't have to turn his head to know Leviathan was coming. Shamayin moved out of his hands, grew out. Strong limbs wound their way up his arm then down his waist. Mal'ak thought this might be more body armor like before, but then it slithered around his legs, constricting, stiffening.

"Wait, what are you doing?" He wanted to scream, but his mouth was completely full of essence. He strove forward with all the strength bestowed to him by the Chronicler, combined with his own, and even then Shamayin overpowered him. He stopped, dead still. By the lines he was a mere fifty-seven cubits from the nearest Dreadnought.

I'm trying to Consume Like the Flame, *you blasted hammer. Let me go,* he screamed silently, beating savagely at the ancient roots holding his hips and legs. Mal'ak was close to the Dreadnought fleet now. They watched in wide eyed terror, not daring to fire a shot, and he could see their beady eyes darting from him to the Shadow of the Deep close on his heels. His stomach churned and the Wyrm in his chest twisted sharply. It was burrowing again. The pain returned tenfold. He could hold it no longer. It didn't matter anyway. The water around him was boiling again. He was close enough—he had to be. All of a sudden, Shamayin thrust onto his face, growing up around his neck and under his eyes, gripping half his face from the muzzle down. Thick wooden fingers pried at his jaws while the root system around his torso and legs squeezed him every bit as hard as the General ever had. He grunted, jaws clenched tight. A drop of essence hung in the crease of his mouth. He did not balk at the pain though, not anymore. He did not struggle anymore either. His Calling, his friends, and his oath, that's all that mattered now. With that, he loosened his jaw. Essence gushed out from between his lips, and as it did, Shamayin went in. Warm essence flowed down his face and gathered, soaking into the hair of his chin. It hung there for a second—a single droplet quavering precariously on the breeze. Everything seemed to move in slow motion. The wind died. Only the boiling sea under his feet danced.

I'll dance with you, he thought with a wry grin. The

Shadow of the Deep overtook him. Leviathan's shade drew halfway into the Dreadnought fleet. Fear was naked on their faces, and he felt resolve etched upon his own. Infinitely more important to them was the essence dangling about his chin. If he hadn't been in so much pain, he would have belly laughed. The truth of it be told, he would have given just about anything to see Tannin's face right about now. Shamayin had apparently reached the Wyrm. It was pulling the filth out of him inch by grueling inch. Light, his chest felt as though it would burst. *Why bother?* he thought. *I'll take the little abomination with me—I'll take them* all *with me.* His eyes cocked a slanted grin at the Dreadfleet. That's all he could move. Soot chugged up from Dreadnought smokestacks; they were running. Mal'ak's eyes squeezed into a smile as the droplet dangling precariously from his chin finally loosed itself, and in its release, he could hear their throaty gasps cast across the open water.

Bloop! One drop, and time seemed to suspend.

130

CHAPTER 8: THE PRECEPTS OF WAR

Shamayin erupted from his throat, wrenching the hairless Wyrm from his body and Leviathan exploded from the depths like a mad titan.

CHAPTER 9:
LEVIATHAN

The Legion fleet splintered in Leviathan's wake. Weapons so formidable against High-Bourne were useless against the Shadow of the Deep. Harpoons and canons lay abandoned, still loaded. "Make for the eye!" Mal'ak heard them shout. Black waves swelled over the Dreadnought decks. "Make for the eye!" they screamed. Terror reigned, and its face was that of Leviathan. The Deep churned into a froth. Mal'ak watched the beast stretch from the ceiling of the Narrows and back into the depths again without revealing its entire length. Dawn's Light, it was massive. And he thought Dragons were big. Dragons were a speck compared to this monster—they all were. Scales as black as soot sliced through the water in front of him. The beast was wrapped from head to tail in plated-scale armor. Only near the head and neck did they thin, giving way to smaller scales that seemed to change color near its mouth. An abyssal hole, bearded with tooth-lined tentacles. Some looked to be the length of the Light bridge back home and some maybe half again. Screams blew across the dark waters with the splintering of Dreadnaught hulls and a low groaning buzz that could only be a Sea Stryder's panic. A whole fleet of them. The waters trembled with their fear. Mal'ak curled up in a ball, clasping his hands over his ears. If Adam would have told him of this creature, Mal'ak doubted he would have believed the telling of it. It was a nightmare straight out of myth. A creature with one master. Who but the Great Lord could stand before this terror? Mal'ak lay huddled on surface tension, coughing in a puddle of his own essence. *So much essence,* he thought. The very thing that the beast desired above all else. The monster dove back into the depths again, sucking down ships too close to the plunge-wake.

Mal'ak swallowed hard, knowing what was next. Through the black and briny murk he could hear it screaming through the depths beneath him, an awful caterwauling, here one second, there the next . . . *Dawn's Light, it's playing with us*, he thought. The sea boiled, filling the Narrows with thick fog. The water beneath him darkened as two yellow lamps turned in the depths toward him. Eyes hungry for angel essence came barreling up from the abyss. The Shadow of the Deep opened its mouth wide beneath him— wide enough to swallow a square block in the celestial city. Mal'ak knew he couldn't escape now, even if he possessed all of his strength. Leviathan's cavernous mouth was a wall of plated teeth. Pieces of the Dreadnought fleet littered its jaws, skewered across the jagged surface. Mal'ak floated on surface tension down, down, down like a gnat in a drain. Adam's Ward still held, for all the good it did against being swallowed alive. Through the fog, a ship floated by, almost sailing over him, its decks full of the doomed, those still not broken or swept overboard hanging on to anything. Down, and down, they all sank into the throat of the beast, until without warning, Mal'ak pitched upward, hanging upside down as the water sank beneath him. "Shamayin!" he gasped, looking at his feet. *Ha! You still hold my legs, you beautiful vine! I could kiss you right now,* he thought. Upside down it was hard to tell, but by the looks of it, Shamayin had grasped onto a toothy outcropping far above. "Don't let go," Mal'ak whispered, patting the vines around his legs. Glancing down into Leviathan's throat, he was just in time to see not one, but two more Dreadnought disappear into the beast's gullet. Quickly, he looked away, but not before something caught his eye, something in the darkness. The hair on Mal'ak's neck bristled. A pale glow shone in the waning light of the Shadow of the Deep's mouth, caught between the cleft of two enormous teeth; an inscription of a Seal.

"By the Silver Cord! A Seal! How did that get here?" Seals were much like Wards, to his recollection, but crafted from magic far more powerful than he'd ever seen. "Seven," he said, staring at the small inscription in front of him. "I remember there are seven of you in the Great Lord's throne room, but . . . why here?" He scratched his chin curiously. Mal'ak had never stopped to think that there was magic in this age powerful enough to manifest a Seal. Magics of the first age, maybe, but not now, and Light, in Leviathan's mouth? Who would dare? It was a death sentence to come here. Ironically, only death could break a Seal's inscription–that was the price, even shadow spawn knew that. It all made very little sense. Another deluge jostled him hard against the plated walls of the beast's mouth, breaking his reverie. Steam rose from his coat as he hung in the darkness. Leviathan was on the move again. "Light of the Dawn Bringer's Blessing!" Mal'ak gripped Shamayin in both hands. "I sound just like him! Here I am . . . stuck in Leviathan's throat with an ancient Seal, and I'm talking to myself in the dark, like I'm not going to die," he said, half grimacing a smile. *The whole thing was absurd. Absurd, unless your eyes are set in ember flame, as golden as a sunrise, and your name is the Chronicler,* he thought.

The shadows moved, stretching out across the roof, like dark fingers. Leviathan was closing his mouth, diving if Mal'ak had to guess.

Light, this is it. At least the High-Bourne are safe. Surely they're making for the eye now. Mal'ak swayed in the darkness, the glow of the Seal barely an arm's length away. Peering down into Leviathan's throat, Mal'ak knuckled his bushy chin, looked sideways at the inscription, then back down again into Leviathan's throat. "Oh, Dawn's Light," he said, biting his lip. "What does it matter, if I'm going to die either way?" Squinting his eyes to slits, he reached out and grabbed it, his whole body clenched like a knot. Slowly he straightened. He cracked one eye, and his brow pulled the other one open as it climbed. The Seal had broken with barely an effort and something sat cold in his hands: a fist sized disc that shimmered like living water, gilded in sapphires and gold weave. It was clasped like a necklace on either side by a woven chain that glinted with the last bit of fading light.

CHAPTER 9: LEVIATHAN

"Dawn Bringer's favor," he said, with a shiver and a grin that pulled at the corners of his mouth. He was too exhausted to muster anything more. "Light knows I shouldn't even be breathing, so why am I surprised to find something in Leviathan's mouth?" He grunted a chuckle that turned into groan. It hurt to laugh now–it hurt to do much of anything. The strong vines of Shamayin still held him aloft, for now. *But for how long?* he thought. *A Dreadnought could drag me down into the beast with it and I wouldn't even see it coming in this darkness. Either way, Seal or no, I am resolved.* Mal'ak shrugged.

It wasn't how he had pictured death, of course. But what a way to go. He shook his head. The necklace somehow widened over his horns, sliding easily around the girth of his neck. Waiting for his end, he closed his eyes and prayed. "Great Lord . . . what a mess I've made of my calling. I don't know how I got here. I don't even see Your hand in it, but I still trust you. It is all I have left to offer, my trust . . . ."

"Come on, Blacksmith!" yelled a voice far above

him. Mal'ak's ears flickered. He craned his head upwards, rubbing his eyes to be sure he wasn't hallucinating. A sliver of light still shone on the far side of Leviathan's cavernous throat. Within that line a silhouette stood betwixt the darkness. Mal'ak's heart soared. The General stood, both hands raised above his head, wings extended. Blue lightning crackled around his broad shoulders as they bulged from the strain.

"Light of the Dawn Bringer!" Mal'ak gaped. "He's holding the beast's jaws open!" Mal'ak's coat pebbled at the site of such courage.

"Come on!" the General yelled again. Mal'ak's arms quivered like untempered steel as he gripped Shamayin's vine. It was slender, but no doubt stronger than any iron that he could have forged back home.

The General snarled through the din, "We are Shade of His Hand, monster! We are *not* prone unto fear! Shadow of the Deep, you cannot have him!"

The General's presence alone seemed to speak life

to Mal'ak's limbs. His head ached, but his heart drummed with a pride he had never felt before. He wiped the bloody brine from his mouth, fixed his eyes on his General, and climbed. Hand over hand, he skittered up Shamayin's tether, surprised at how quickly the top approached. Cresting the last plated tooth, he crouched in between the space the General was holding open for him. The General gritted his teeth, his bronze arms trembling from the pressure of Leviathan's jaws.

"Jump!"

Mal'ak leaped from the Shadow of the Deep's mouth. His ear drums distorted at the beast's caterwauling. The surface of the Narrows barreled up at him, striking with bone jarring force, but again Adam's Ward held him fast just above the surface. The General's body plummeted into the water beside him like an angelic missile, but surfaced immediately.

"Run, Blacksmith. Make for the eye. Run!"

"I'm not leaving you," Mal'ak said, surprised by the

steadiness in his voice. "Besides, I don't think my legs are working very well."

The General scanned him up and down, quickly weighing the options. Mal'ak's left hoof was split through, up the side—probably from the impact. A growl escaped the General's lips.

"Give me your cloak. Hurry!"

Mal'ak slipped it from around his shoulders. As soon as the fabric left his hands, he slipped neck deep into the boiling black liquid. It burned, even through his thick coat. If it burned the General, Mal'ak could not tell.

"We'll be boiled alive out here."

"No, we will not," the General said, climbing onto the surface of the Deep with Mal'ak's cloak wrapped around his thigh. Leviathan had submerged again. "He's coming. Hold on, Blacksmith." With that, he lifted Mal'ak up under his arm. They moved so swiftly across the water that at first, Mal'ak thought they were flying. Leviathan's shadow faded as they careened toward the Eye of the Maelstrom.

CHAPTER 9: LEVIATHAN

The sleek bodied Sea Stryders were already cresting the wall of the vortex. They had overtaken the larger, slower Dreadnaught fleet, their agile frames ramping up on waves, sending them airborne thirty cubits in their haste. The Dread fleet mixed with the Stryders, chugging out black soot, pushing right through the massive waves that the Stryders were jumping. No shots were fired. No attack was mounted from any vessel, Stryder or Dreadnought. Eternal enemies sailed side by side as fast as they could, desperate with one central hope—survival.

"I don't see him," Mal'ak yelled through the howling wind.

"He cannot pass into the Eye," the General said as he sped forward. "Even the World Breaker has boundaries. But keep an eye trained. His Shadow will cast where he's about to strike." The rim of the Maelstrom rose before them both, a hydrous, swirling storm that dwarfed even the World Breaker. The Eye of the Maelstrom churned inverted lightning into a slow spin, dragging both fleets inexorably toward the center, toward the ragged edges of time. Without warning, shadow darkened the stygian waters behind them, and the depths grew hoary, boiling with that awful caterwauling. Leviathan had not surfaced yet, but even now Mal'ak could hear the beast's muffled wailing. Fear stabbed at his gut. *If death had a scream, this would be it*, thought Mal'ak. He looked toward the Eye of the Maelstrom, then back to the monstrous shadow closing in on them, and his heart sank. The lines in his head told the story. The Beast *would* close the gap before they reached the Eye. They simply were not going to make it. The General *had* to know this, even without a Crafter's spacial gift, but he ran anyway.

"Take hold of courage," the General said, his voice barely heard over the roar of the waves. There was no panic, only single-minded determination.

"But we're not going to make it!" yelled Mal'ak. "The Dawn preserve us!" Suddenly, a cold snap bit his chest, like he had stuffed ice down his tunic. Out of instinct, he clutched at it, inadvertently grabbing something hanging about his neck. "The Amulet," he said, goggle eyed. It had changed. The golden disc that shimmered like living water, gilded in sapphires and gold weave, was cold to the touch, now ice-blue and swirling. All at once, the water underneath the General's feet swelled, swirling, surging forward in a wave. Mal'ak stared at the amulet, then at the water pushing them forward. Hope sprang up inside of him. It wasn't exactly courage, but it was *something*. He had no idea how the amulet worked, or if it had anything to do with the wave beneath them, but he held it in both hands anyway, willing the water to go faster, trying to combine its speed with the General's stride. Gently, the black waters rose higher—higher and faster.

"It's working!" said Mal'ak, half amazed, half still terrified. The General was running, but his stride fell on the crest of the wave brought to life by the Amulet in Mal'ak's hands. Mal'ak could be amazed another day that the waters obeyed the amulet. Today, he wanted to go faster—he wanted to live. Squeezing his eyes shut, he squeezed the amulet and prayed. "Faster. Burn you, *please*, go faster." The black waters rose even higher, even faster, and the caterwauling began to fade. He opened his eyes . . . the shadow was fading too. Then just like that, it was gone.

Mal'ak exhaled, but the General kept running without a word, the strain on his face evidence that the beast was not done yet. His wings lay flat against his back and his legs were a blur as he ran toward the Eye of the Maelstrom. Without warning or slowing stride, he wrapped both of his arms around Mal'ak and launched seventy cubits into the air. From the deep, darkness ascended. Leviathan exploded from the depths underneath them. Mal'ak gritted his teeth, closing his tufted ears flat against his head, but still that caterwauling scream swept across the waters, rattling his ears. Had the General not leapt, they would have surely been swallowed outright—and might still. Angel and Aspect barreled through the air. Mal'ak looked back, but quickly wished he hadn't. Leviathan's cavernous mouth was agape. The sheer girth of it made Mal'ak feel as if they were already within the rim of its toothy maw again. Hot breath blew his fur back as tentacles strained from the beast's beard, reaching for them. Worse still, Mal'ak could measure the exact dimensions of the Shadow of the Deep's mouth and the rapidly diminishing distance between it and them with gut wrenching clarity. Sometimes, he hated being a Crafter.

"We're not going to make it. Dawn preserve us," Mal'ak said, bracing himself. As if in answer, the beast's head thrashed violently from side to side. It screamed, straining his ear drums close to bursting, then faded into the distance almost as quickly as it had come upon them.

"The Eye!" the General yelled. "Don't let go."

Mal'ak tightened his grip and felt the General tighten his as they tumbled end over end, falling, falling, falling. The General's wings clung tightly against his back. He dared not open them yet—not here, never here. If they caught sail here, on the winds of time's frayed edges, they could be whisked away to who knows where, or worse, to who knows when.

No wonder no one ever flies in the Narrows, thought

Mal'ak. *Only a fool would take wing here.* The moment hung in the air, quiet, eerily quiet. A Sea Stryder floated by, or half of its bow, the terror of Leviathan perfectly preserved on its once beautiful face. Mal'ak shivered. *Thank the Great Lord it was not Oniya.* The Maelstrom drew them forward like a hungry mouth, yet they seemed to slow the closer they drew toward the center, like a stretching of all things.

Mal'ak remembered the Chronicler's words: *"It is the Great Lord's own hand that stirs the chronal waters of the Deep and beyond."*

Mal'ak knew without asking that they rode upon the very wake of His fingertips—the last wave. He wasn't sure if angels were supposed to see this sort of thing. Especially Ta'ow. It was disorienting. Simple things like falling didn't feel like falling anymore, and Light only knew which way was up or down. The only sure direction was the Eye; the only direction that mattered. In the end, it was gravity that grabbed them, pulling on their limbs as surely as if tethered by a rope. Everything came together—a soup of celestial bodies, poured through a great hole in the sky, the Eye of the Maelstrom. The General was silent concentration, jaw set like flint, and his body as tense as a drawn bow. He adjusted his grip around Mal'ak's waist, then twisted in midair without warning. The archangel maneuvered his body like something born to fly, careful not to unfurl his great wings to the winds. He folded them in close, gently encircling them both. Mal'ak gasped as the General's feathers grew hot, changing before Mal'ak's eyes into bladed plates, dense, and hard—like a broad blade pulled from one of his forge furnaces back home. Glowing, they formed a wall of plated embers—a winged shield. The only shield either one of them had.

Mal'ak held his breath as time reclaimed the moment in a brutal embrace; its governing laws ripped them from the heavens like a bolt of lightning. He must have blacked out for a moment, because when he came to, his head was spinning. The Wyrm, Leviathan, and the loss of so much essence had apparently taken more out of him than he cared to admit. He heard digging, and felt the General's strong arm still a little too tight around his waist.

He never let me go, Mal'ak thought, exhausted but relieved. The General crawled out of a hole in the ground, into the moonlight, hauling Mal'ak up by the scruff of his neck and set him on the rim of the crater they had apparently just made. Cloudless twilight revealed silhouettes coming out of the ground everywhere, all scurrying for cover as soon as their feet were firmly under them again. Those with wings and strong enough took to the air. Those on foot ran in whatever direction they did not see an enemy. The General gave Mal'ak a once over, then reached out to the High-Bourne tribes through the link.

"Regroup, no less than twos. Rune-Craft will be needed. Those with the talent for healing, rally to the Chronicler."

Mal'ak's ears perked straight up. He wasn't sure how the General knew, or could know, that the Chronicler was alive and well, but that news was the best he'd heard since leaving the Great Lord's Kingdom, and the relief that filled him was almost equal to his exhaustion. He smiled, thinking of Adam. He would have to remember to tell him that he had just found a brand new favorite day. He had grown quite fond of the elder High-Bourne and the General, if he were completely honest.

Mal'ak did not bother the General with any more questions today. He was busy, already barking out orders to the tribes. For the moment, Mal'ak was content to just sit. For the moment he would rest. They had made it and that was enough. *By the Silver Cord, they had made it.* But made it where?

CHAPTER 10: THE GATHERING

Mal'ak tugged nervously at the hair on his chin, then caught himself in the act. The Wyrm was gone, of course, but the habit remained—sort of. At least he wasn't scratching his neck now. *A new habit to go with a new emotion, for an even newer occasion,* he thought with a grin. Though there were no words for *this* occasion. Not really. How could anyone fashion words to fit the Epoch Horizon? For the moment, he would happily have settled for an explanation on how he actually fit into this world. *How does a perfect being assimilate imperfect emotions?* He knuckled his forehead, puzzling over how the High-Bourne seemed so adept at managing fallen emotions on earth. His time here had been short since leaving the Narrows. Most days, new emotions came at him almost rapid fire. It was a chore just to assimilate them all, much less write them all down in his journal. Most of the time he felt happy to be here—even thrilled, when he wasn't being chased by giant Aspects and throwing up Wyrms, that is. But then there always seemed to be something new to wrestle with down here. This very moment he wrestled with what the General called "nerves," which apparently brought on this involuntary reaction of tugging at the chin, even without the Wyrm.

"Nerves," the General had explained, "are troublesome things you have to grow accustomed to here in the dominion of humans."

For Mal'ak, this was proving to be quite true. He had never known a nervous moment in his life under the Lion banner. Of course, where the Great Lord ruled there was no Blight and emotions like nerves simply did not exist. The mere thought of them, there in that place, was as absurd as it was alien to him here and now, in this place. He had at least sorted out that nerves were not quite the same thing as fear. Mal'ak knew fear intimately now, experienced it outright in the Narrows. How could you be part of the High-Bourne and *not* be acquainted with it? He had fought the shadow side by side with Archistrategos—the General himself, and survived battles that, Light help him, he thought would be impossible to live through.

A baptism by fire, the General called it. "Knowledge is better kindled through the fires of experience," he would say in his booming tone that no one ever seemed to question. As far as nerves were concerned, Mal'ak felt they had a more subtle effect on the mind than the machinations of outright fear. Still, he was not very fond of either. However, he absolutely loved chin pulling. It was so . . . *human*. Grabbing a quill and parchment from his pocketed pack, Mal'ak began scribbling the details of this emotion called nerves the best he could. He was so excited to finally pen out this marvelous new discovery of chin pulling, he could hardly write fast enough. *I have to ask Adam,* he thought, ears fidgeting. *What do humans do with this odd emotion?* Mal'ak's fascination with Adam's seed grew by the day. The endless conversations they had shared in the Great Lord's Kingdom did not do his children justice—not to Mal'ak. Nothing was like the Haze of earth. When not training, he set his heart to understanding them better. He desired to know their fears and of faith. He desired to know of his Lord's great love for humans. *Love* was the pinnacle, as far as he was concerned. And though he had not had the chance yet, he was sure he could spend an entire human lifetime watching a single family love their way through this imperfect world. Many nights he would venture into the small, dirt village, not far from the High-Bourne encampment, just to watch Adam's children, especially the families. Why, for love's sake alone, it could take him years to settle on a proper theorem to measure the complexities of *human* love played out in a family. It was so different from the Great Lord's all-encompassing Love that he had known in heaven. But make no mistake . . . it was still love, and it seemed to grow over a period of time. Its depth matured with the passing of time, depth Mal'ak was unable to measure as yet, despite his abilities as a Crafter. But it seemed rooted in purposed affection and a sustained bond of earned trust, as he understood it. It was fascinating, but his favorite part had to be the wondrous way that human love could exist upon an instant, in full bloom! Angels did not bear children, so to Mal'ak, childbirth was an earthbound marvel. Adam and Eve's children could *choose* to bring a life into this world. *Life, of all things*, thought Mal'ak.

Of all of the Great Lord's gifts, and in all of the realms, was there another gift so lavish? That sons and daughters of clay could *make* life. And when they did, when a man and woman saw their daughter or son born into the world, it was as if love was born into the world with it. Mal'ak's ears fluttered furiously at the notion. This was exactly the opposite of the man and woman's love for each other. Their love for each other seemed to grow over time,

157

but the love for their baby was instant. No merit, nothing earned or deserved, just . . . instantaneous love, not based on what the child had accomplished, but entirely upon *whose* he or she was. It reminded Mal'ak of the Father. Of course *no* love was truly like the Great Lord's, but the pattern was unmistakable. He wondered if it had even occurred to humans the beautiful parallel they shared with the Great Lord, that every time one of their own children was born into the world, love undeserved was born again as well. *Such an obvious correlation,* he mused. He scribbled furiously, surprised he had not noticed it before now.

I'm doing it again, he thought with a smile. *Next, I might sprout wings, and my limbs might start moving independently of themselves if I keep spending so much time with the Chronicler.* "Indeed," he said, giving a curt sniff, then laughing to himself.

Mal'ak had to push these and other thoughts to the side for now. There was so much to think and journal about, but he had to set his mind to the task the General had laid out for him. Quickly, he stuffed the quill and parchment back into his pack and once more looked upon a sight he knew could make even an archangel nervous.

Since time began, this was a first. Never before had the Great Lord gathered so great a number. The Narrows had dumped them all here, except humans. Against hope, Mal'ak had scanned the crowd for days and everyone's patience had suffered to the point of irritation by him asking so much, but Adam was nowhere to be found. In fact, not a single human came to the Haze, as far as he could tell. But when *all* angels and *all* demons gather in one number, and in one place, who could say? It was quite a sight, though. They veiled the horizon like a shroud, touching the boundaries of earth's atmosphere, then fanned outward across the stars as far as he could see. To say the journey through the Narrows had left both parties edgy would be a colossal understatement. Even the higher caste seemed on edge. *Of course, the assemblage of this kind of power would test the nerve of anyone, save the Great Lord himself,* thought Mal'ak. Some of the angels gathered here were so high in rank, that no demon had ever seen since the Age of the Turning, angels rumored about in fearful whispers, deep within the strongholds of Baal-Shadow. Strangely, Mal'ak could not remember a single one of the higher caste coming through the Narrows. The General had kept him so busy with the Precepts of War, he had little time to notice much, but here they were, at the Epoch Horizon, bright as a sunrise. He was still awed by the sight of them. The regal Seraphim or Fiery Ones, as they were called back home. These angels offer to the Great Lord the glory of an eternal song. Mal'ak smiled. He loved the idea of a forever song, he just couldn't wrap his head around the forging of it. *How do you craft a melody and lyric that is always new and never ends?* He shook his head at the wonder of it, then became distracted by the Seraphim's wheels. To Mal'ak, Seraphim wheels were a wonder in and of themselves. Round, blue spheres of sentient energy ripe for Ta'ow study as far as he was concerned. He still didn't know what the round wheel casings were made of, but lightning latticed the inner workings of their bodies as they flew, and they always flew in tandem with the Seraphim. In fact, to Mal'ak's recollections, the Seraphim are never without their wheeled consorts—ever. Wherever the Seraphim are, the Wheels within wheels are sure to follow. Mal'ak had pondered about the relationship between the two for ages. His journal pages were full of theorems about the Seraphim and the mysterious Wheels within wheels. Until now, he had never seen them away from the Great Lord's presence, and never in a setting like this. They hovered beside their Wheels, just above the ground, wings drumming the air effortlessly. They were still his absolute favorite, with that never ending song and those wings, Dawn's Light! Nothing had wings like the Seraphim. Six diaphanous wings pointed skyward out of thick muscular sides, reaching far above his head. They spanned Mal'ak's height by four and half again at their apex. And the awareness they afforded would make a High-Bourne green with envy. Nothing in all the realms could sneak up on the Seraphim—though Mal'ak was hard pressed to think of any demon crazy enough to try and sneak up on an angel whose wings were full of eyes. He had counted at least a thousand, and that was by twilight. Abruptly, his tufted ears perked straight up, concern rolling the fur above his brow in tight rows. He looked around, wondering if anyone else noticed . . . the Seraphim were silent!

"Another first," Mal'ak muttered. It was a hush he could almost feel. *Why would the Seraphim quiet the eternal song?* He tugged his chin hair a little harder, watching them hover there, silent as the grave. Every single one of their eyes fixed hard upon the demonic throng camped merely one thousand cubits away. This had to set many a hell demon at unease, especially those among the front lines. *Dawn knows those eyes are making some demon tug on his chin somewhere.* Mal'ak managed a toothy grin as he scanned the multitude. The Seraphim were here, the Elders, the Powers, the Living Creatures, and the mighty Cherubim, all encamped about the tiny little town. "By the Silver Cord!" Mal'ak muttered. "I bet the throne room is empty."

CHAPTER 10: THE GATHERING

'*That is correct,*' the Chronicler's voice chimed through the link. '*We are all here, even your favorite, the Seraphim.*' Mal'ak sensed amusement in the Chronicler's tone, or sensed it through the link. Mal'ak's cheeks flushed. Apparently, he'd forgotten to drop the link . . . *again.* The Chronicler was nowhere around, or at least nowhere that Mal'ak could see. It was embarrassingly easy to forget that you shared head space with someone through the link, especially when that someone quietly travels out of range for a while. Once back in range, the tether that bound their minds reconnects, like it had never broken connection. It made sense, in a strange way. After all, the link was more of a latent gift than anything else. Something that was felt, more than learned. Mal'ak had never experienced the like, even in heaven. Normally, he loved it. Already the pages of his journal had captured much of the experience.

A collective consciousness, seven minds deep, never more than seven. Any more, and the link became muddled, especially concurrent thought. It was efficient in communication, efficient in

communal bonding and especially efficient in combat. Thoroughly High-Bourne, he noted. Though at the moment, it was more embarrassing than it was anything. Come to think of it . . . he might just leave that part out.

At least the Chronicler's amusement seemed to be rooted in endearment more than anything, but it was still embarrassing.

Light. Thoughts lay as bare as a newborn when you open yourself to the link. He was just thankful the General wasn't listening in, at least Mal'ak didn't sense him listening. Of course, now the Chronicler was privy to these thoughts as well. Mal'ak swallowed awkwardly, trying to salvage any dignity left in the moment.

"The Dragon were Cherubim once, weren't they?"

"Indeed," said the Chronicler. "And I imagine a Ta'ow like yourself would want to be privy to how it all happened? For your journal," he added quickly, with a small quirk to his mouth.

"Well, I'm a really good listener," said Mal'ak. "If

you're of a mind to tell me . . . of the war that is." Mal'ak could have sworn there was a flash through the link, something about Ta'ow curiosity, but then it disappeared. He felt a little guilty for asking. A little . . . but not enough to keep him from the question. He could feel the Chronicler's countenance sink without so much as a glimpse of the archangel's face, the link shimmered, memories rippled like rings across a pond, and Mal'ak knew he had stepped into sadness—a deep pool that spanned ages. "It's okay if you would rather not talk of it," said Mal'ak, having second thoughts. "I don't know much. The Ta'ow never saw the battlefield, but we were touched by the war just the same, even in heaven."

"We all were," the Chronicler said, suddenly appearing. "High-Bourne became War-Bound, blacksmiths became weapon-smiths. In fact, Ta'ow kilns gave birth to some of our most powerful weapons this side of the Turning."

"Is that how Shamayin came to be?"

"I don't know."

"*You* don't know?" Mal'ak's brow raised in genuine disbelief.

"There are many things beyond me," the Chronicler said, chuckling. "The Dawn only knows, but considering the source, Shamayin could have been forged for an entirely different purpose. I would not be surprised if it were somehow forged solely for you," he said with a wink. "But you would have to ask the Aspects to know for sure, and we've already seen what *one* of them can do in the Narrows." He shuddered. "Now, as to your *original* question. The truth is, the war gave rise to many changes. We did stand against the Dragon in the first and greatest battle the realms have ever known."

"But you won, right? Everything is good . . . you won," said Mal'ak.

"Victory was ours *that* day, yes. But Light of the Dawn . . . there were moments, moments when a perfect mind can be a perfect curse. Moments that I wish I could forget, like the humans do. Moments spent wondering if there would be anything left when this war was done. We scorched the heavens with God Almighty's wrath, Mal'ak. All these planets you see?" The Chronicler spread out his hands toward the stars. "They were framed in beauty, like earth, and then we burned them all to ash. To *win* ... we laid waste to creation, save one place—earth."

"I didn't know," Mal'ak said, stunned. "So many planets ... "

"Yes. War does not discriminate between who bleeds, and we all bled that day in one way or another. And the loss of High-Bourne was beyond the count of sorrows. But victory was ours that day, the Dawn Bringer be praised. And we gained a General of generals in the process," the Chronicler said with a quick nod. "As you can well imagine, he made the Dragon's fall *particularly* painful."

Mal'ak was a little surprised at the sudden amount of satisfaction filtering through the link. The Chronicler's face was polished stone, but inside the link, the memory burned with righteous justice being served.

Mal'ak could still remember the rumors of those days. Stories of the General and the High-Bourne would now and then reach the celestial city, and he *lived* for these stories. He would often wait for the messengers by the Pearl Gate, just to hear the news first.

"Is that when they started calling him Archistrategos?" Mal'ak said wide eyed.

"Why yes, I suppose it is. Unfortunately," the Chronicler paused deep in thought. "Our General was not the only one to rise to prominence in that age. Another rose, a hell-spawn from the pit of Baal-Shadow itself."

"The Death demon, Samyaza?" Mal'ak said, breathlessly.

"Yes, lord of the Fallen."

The fur on the nape of Mal'ak's neck prickled. War stories could run wild over time, especially when they had ages to grow, and Samyaza and his Grigori were tied to almost all of the worst ones.

"Can you tell me of him?" Mal'ak said, with more excitement in his voice than he'd meant to show, but then remembered the link and sighed.

"I can tell you the Grigori are cunning and resourceful and only number about two hundred. They are *never* to be underestimated Mal'ak . . . *never*. They fell from a higher caste than us, and still, their influence is considerable. There is no doubt that their reach is far beyond their prison of Baal-Shadow. Their touch is even felt by man. Wise is the High-Bourne who treads carefully when dealing with the Grigori, Mal'ak . . . wise indeed."

"Are they here? Did Samyaza come to the Epoch Horizon?"

The Chronicler nodded for him to follow. "He is clothed in shadow, so there will not be much to see, if we see him at all."

Mal'ak nodded, knuckling his chin furiously, while fumbling through the pockets of his pack for quill and parchment.

They strode behind the front lines. Most of the High-Bourne were perched in twos. Some were in trees, and some were scattered in the high nooks and crannies of the mountains. And that was just the ones that were uncloaked—

the ones who wanted to be seen. Most of them crouched silently, bodies as tense as a bow string, motionless, except for that sweeping motion of their heads. *The Precepts of War,* thought Mal'ak.

By the lines in his head, he knew they had traveled laterally two thousand and one hundred cubits north by northwest. He had followed the Chronicler's steady gait easily enough and even had to slow his stride a bit to not pull ahead. *Being Ta'ow does have some advantages.* He smiled to himself, though he would have bartered his stature for a set of High-Bourne wings any day.

The front lines were thick with artillery, most of which Mal'ak had never seen before. They seemed based on a design to harness light. Come to think of it, until now, he had not realized the High-Bourne had made most of them, if not all of them. Alone in the Haze, ages might have passed, but eventually they would have had to design their own weapons. Some were a bit crude, but that was understandable without a Ta'ow's hammer and anvil.

CHAPTER 10: THE GATHERING

Mal'ak grinned satisfactorily. He had to admit, some of it was outright genius. Weapons based on light were weapons that could not be used or prosper against them.

"You approve?" the Chronicler said, interrupting his thoughts. "It's ok, you can be candid, Mal'ak." He tapped his forehead.

Mal'ak sighed. "I know . . . the link."

"Our artisans would like a word with you, when time permits. They could make good use of your gifting. The weapons they have engineered for the war have been effective, but it seems they do not possess the skill to give shape to the words of God as the Ta'ow forgers of your clans can—as *you* can. It seems they lack the necessary finesse of a Crafter's touch."

"It's more of a forging process really," Mal'ak said, feeling his cheeks begin to flush again, noticing that the Chronicler called him "Crafter" and not "Blacksmith." For some reason, he'd almost grown fond of the way the General referred to him as "Blacksmith." Admiration rose through the link, warm and friendly—the Chronicler's admiration. Mal'ak looked up into those ancient eyes, held in golden flame, then down again, fiddling with his chin.

"You are surprised? Surprised that I admire something you have?" the Chronicler asked, with a quirked smile.

Mal'ak's brow rose, and he felt something else pulsing through the link. Pulsing in a rhythm, like laughter, like—humor?

"By the Silver Cord! you're enjoying this," Mal'ak said, half indignant.

The Chronicler's mouth rounded into a full blown smile with teeth. "It is why we love you, Mal'ak. It is why everyone does. In a fallen world, time and war will leave its mark where you least expect—on the inside of you. Time may not wear our skin, but here in the Haze, attrition is her slow and steady sword. Though we may be undiminished on the outside, in the Haze of earth, even a perfect heart can grow weary. And then there's you," he said, kindly. "A

Ta'ow, our scouts find on the battlefield, all alone, with his head thrown back singing, *singing* like Dragons and the war of the ages does not even exist. Even *here* your mind drifts, Mal'ak. We stand at the brink of war this very moment, and your mind drifts toward High-Bourne wings and bartered stature, weapons and who knows what else will pass through that bull-head of yours."

Abruptly, two High-Bourne sentries approached, who might as well have been twin statues for all the emotion conveyed on those stone faces. Without warning, they stopped, snapped two fists across their chests and saluted. At first, Mal'ak assumed they were saluting the Chronicler, but their second fisted salute was aimed right at him. Whispers of Leviathan and Ruwach-Latash reached his ears. And then another two sentries uncloaked.

"Ruwach-Latash," they said, saluting plain as noonday.

Mal'ak's ears wilted. "Dawn's Light!" he whispered. "They're saluting *me*. They're calling me . . . ."

"Ruwach-Latash. *Spirit-Forger*," said the Chronicler,

stopping in his tracks. "It seems you have already earned a new name among us." A determinedness solidified across the link. "They are only responding to what they see in you. To what we all see in you. It is an honor, Mal'ak, one that can take centuries, if not millennia, to achieve, and sometimes a new name is never achieved. Some never survive long enough to gain a new name."

"A new name? Me?"

"Yes," said the Chronicler. "A Ta'ow Crafter, running across the Narrows to face the Shadow of the Deep, *alone*. You saved us all, Mal'ak," he said with a firm nod of his head. "That is one of the bravest acts I have ever seen."

If Mal'ak's face was warm before, it felt as hot as his kiln back home now.

"But why would they give me a new name when I brought the Wyrm into our midst in the first place?" he asked sheepishly. "It was the least I could do on my oath as a High-Bourne. I'm not afraid to die . . . ."

The Chronicler raised a hand. "Well . . ." he sniffed.

"About that—dying that is—there are far worse things in this place than dying. You would do well to remember this. Some would see dying as mercy's sweetest embrace."

All of a sudden, Mal'ak sensed something flicker across the link. A face, or image of a face, but it was gone before he could catch a good glimpse. Trying to track concurrent thought through an archangel's mind was like tracking the ripples of a river. One thought bled into the next, and the next, and the next, too many to keep track of. One thing however, came through clearly. That face was attached to a sadness that Mal'ak could feel inside his bones, and it sat at the very bottom of a deep pool of memory.

"There is something I should have told you about the Aspects," the Chronicler said, deliberately directing their thoughts in a different direction. "Leviathan is one of four Aspects that manifested in an age without age. In the Narrows, the Crafters of the high mountains call the Aspects by a different name. The Daq of the North call them the Unmade." He paused, as if to weigh the sum of his words.

"They, like the Leviathan, were brought forth from another pattern, something that is beyond our kind—far beyond immortals. The Great Lord framed them all this way, for reasons that remain His own, and before you ask . . . I do not know *why*," he said, continuing on, like Mal'ak's mouth wasn't sitting wide open, poised for a question. "Therefore, opinions are speculative," he sniffed. "Our most proficient think-wells postulate from piecemeal information. They think the Aspects are of a higher caste. *Personally,* I do not adhere to this point of view," he sniffed again, sharply, and mild irritation glimmered across the link.

"Then what are they?" said Mal'ak.

"I am not sure. That they predate the Ages and even the current universe, suggests that they are not angels. Maybe they *are* of a higher caste, but they are *not* angels. Maybe they are *expressions* of something entirely different. So little is known, it is folly to hazard more than a guess."

"So . . . what if something happened and you *had* to hazard more than a guess, what do you *think* they could be?"

CHAPTER 10: THE GATHERING

Mal'ak said, his tufted ears fidgeting with Ta'ow curiosity. His hand had been itching to go for his quill and parchments since the conversation began, but the Chronicler's thin lipped stare and raised brow, made him think better of it. Mal'ak had learned by now that two brows raised by the Chronicler usually meant pleasant surprise, quickly followed by a brief porcelain smile. One brow raised, however, was . . . well, not good—not through the link anyway. "Ahem," the Chronicler cleared his throat through pursed lips. "I have *already* told you what I believe them *not* to be, and as yet, we simply do not know what they are. Beyond that is a mystery. Indeed, for all our diligence, *mystery* seems to be our defining reward concerning the Aspects. And as you have seen, it is far too dangerous to approach them to find out more. Despite our best efforts, we know precious little of Leviathan or of the other Aspects. But this we do know, dear Mal'ak—whatever Leviathan consumes, becomes . . . *unmade.*" He paused, letting the words sink in. "He doesn't just eat your body, Mal'ak, he consumes all that you are and

177

ever were. To be devoured by the Shadow of the Deep is to never have been."

Mal'ak's mouth fell open, and a lump formed in the top of his throat. "You mean—he came back for me," Mal'ak said, stopping dead in his tracks not bothering to pull at his chin. "The General came back for me, and *you* . . . you both risked *everything*—for me?"

The Chronicler shushed him with a sharp sniff. "Is your Calling Sacrosanct?"

Mal'ak nodded.

"Then how, under the light, could we *not* follow you?" the Chronicler asked with the softest smile Mal'ak had ever seen on a High-Bourne. "*We* are Shade of His Hand," he said, touching Mal'ak's chest with an open palm. "*High-Bourne.* And in all the ages, I have *never* seen anything *more* High-Bourne than you running across that water. I thought the General's chest would burst from pride when you leaped over that rail." The Chronicler chuckled with a shake of his head.

CHAPTER 10: THE GATHERING

"But I don't deserve it . . . ."

"Of course you don't," the Chronicler snapped. "Why on earth do you think you were chosen for it?" He winked.

"You sound like Adam," Mal'ak said, rolling his eyes as a few more High-Bourne snapped their salutes in passing.

"Ok, we are close." The Chronicler's voice came to a whisper. "There," he pointed his finger. "The General's scouts report Samyaza is cloaked beyond those dales, just north of those hills."

By the lines in Mal'ak's head, he was pointing sixty-six degrees northwest. A stiff breeze blew in from the north, wafting in the stench of sulfur.

"I don't see him," Mal'ak whispered, his mouth watering with nausea.

"Let your eyes adjust. There, in the cleft of those boulders. There, you see?"

The wind stirred again, stirred all but the blackness in that bare cleft of rock, stirred all but the archdemon himself. In the end, that is what gave him away. Not movement, but the lack of it.

"The winds do not stir Samyaza," whispered the Chronicler. "He is a shadow amongst shadows."

Finally, he did move, arms and legs rolling beneath liquid darkness. Mal'ak caught a quick glimpse of his hand exposed, gaunt and thin, and a portion of his face that looked more like dried flax stretched thin over pale bone.

"Eve!" Mal'ak whispered. "Did you see that? Its face just changed. It looks like Eve now."

"Yes, it rarely reveals itself, but when it does, it is sometimes in her likeness."

"Why?" asked Mal'ak, finding a handful of chin hair.

"I do not know that either," the Chronicler said, pursing his lips. "But if I had to guess, I would say it is gloating. For who of womanly beauty could ever rival the likeness of Eve? I believe it gloats in his triumph over her, Mal'ak. I believe that it mocks Eden's end, which was precisely the beginning of its reign."

"Adam would be so—*mad*," said Mal'ak, his hands

clenching into fists.

"Indeed. I imagine he would be."

"I would know *more*," Mal'ak said flatly.

The Chronicler looked off in the distance, then to Mal'ak again. "Yes, I suppose *you* would," he said, with a sliver of amusement flashing through the link. "Let's make our way back, and I will tell you what I can."

Memories suddenly flooded the link, as the archangel gathered his thoughts. Images flashed, some brutal, some terrifying.

"We slew him that day," he said, staring at the stars. "Samyaza, and many others. The few Grigori that survived, we chased from the heavens. Samyaza's essence was absorbed into the realm of Baal-Shadow, like all of the demon dead.

Mal'ak shivered. No angel dared venture into that place. Not even archangels.

"We thought we had seen the last of the Grigori leader, but eventually he rose again.

"But that's impossible," said Mal'ak in disbelief.

"Indeed. Apparently for all but Samyaza. Baal-Shadow did hold him for a time, so—he *was* dead, technically, or dead as we knew it at the time, which left the Grigori leaderless for a time. Without his leadership, they grew bold in their wickedness, and dared too much. They broke the Prime Command, Mal'ak. They transgressed against the Great Lord himself."

Mal'ak kept his silence. Of course, breaking the Prime Command was sacrilege. You don't mess with the free will of man. That was God and God alone's province. That was a line he was pretty sure Lucifer had never even crossed.

"The price for their trespass was banishment," the Chronicler continued. "We hunted them for centuries. It took centuries to capture them all, but eventually we did. They were cast into outer darkness alive, into Baal-Shadow, where the Great Lord Himself inscribed a Seal upon their tomb. To this day, their tomb is still sealed, as far as we know."

"But . . . I don't understand," said Mal'ak. "If Seals

cannot be broken except by death, then how did Samyaza escape?" he asked, absentmindedly tracing the outline of the small disc with his finger through his tunic.

"With knowledge that is too great," the Chronicler said, flashing his golden eyes to Mal'ak's hand.

Mal'ak grimaced, hoping the link had not given up his secret. Well, he'd not kept it a *secret*—not exactly. He tried bringing it up several times, but both the General and the Chronicler had not stopped since the beginning of the campaign. Besides, the amulet needed to be studied, and since he was the only Crafter present—well, he was just *curious*, that's all. But not overly curious, *never* that.

"Ahem," the Chronicler sniffed.

Mal'ak blinked with a start, jerking his hand away from the amulet.

"As I was saying . . . there is knowledge that is too great, and I'll get to that, and Samyaza in a moment. But you should know, that amulet hanging about your neck is something else entirely. It is called the Tetragrammaton, and its legend predates the Age of the Turning. Only four pieces exist. Even the Elders speak of the hallowed-four in veiled whispers. The pieces are bound to Him, Mal'ak, bound to the Great Lord as surely as the one hanging about your neck is bound to your sacred Calling. As for the other three, I cannot say.

Mal'ak let out a sigh. "Why are Callings always tied to things that hurt?" he said, knowing he hadn't fooled anyone—not with that blasted link. The Chronicler opened his mouth, then pursed his lips thoughtfully.

"Well now . . . that *is* an interesting question, and an honest assessment of Callings, I suppose."

"It is?" asked Mal'ak.

"Indeed. A wise and sober earth observation. But it really deserves more thought than we have time to allow. You would do well to ponder on it later, though."

Mal'ak beamed a toothy grin, while scribbling down his very first *wisdom* quote.

Why are Callings always tied to . . .

184

CHAPTER 10: THE GATHERING

"Mal'ak," the Chronicler said, putting his hand on the parchment. Compassion and a little impatience flittered through the link. "We have precious little time to discuss your original queries concerning Samyaza, much less the Oracle hanging about your neck." The Chronicler met Mal'ak's eyes with a steely seriousness. "Keep it close to you, and the Great Lord willing, your Calling will take care of the rest." Mal'ak bobbed a nod, still grinning, amazed that he said something that the Chronicler deemed worthy of calling *wise*. "As I was saying," the Chronicler took a deep breath. "There is knowledge that is too great, knowledge that was never meant to be obtained by some."

"Forbidden knowledge?" said Mal'ak.

"Yes."

"How?" Mal'ak exhaled in relief, trying not to think about the amulet anymore.

"By consulting with the Aspect, Urim, that is how."

"Dawn's Light, Lucifer spoke with *another* Aspect?" asked Mal'ak. Then his ears slowly wilted to his cheeks.

"I . . .I still don't understand."

"The camp is not far now," the Chronicler continued. "I will try to finish, but I must warn you, knowledge can often lead to more questions than answers. Such is the way of knowledge. Do you understand?"

Mal'ak nodded eagerly.

"It began in secret, with the whispers of two mad demons deep within the bowels of Baal-Shadow. There, a tenuous pact was struck between Lucifer and Samyaza that would give both what they so desperately desired."

"They worked together?" Mal'ak asked.

"Yes. Lucifer gained the forbidden knowledge of the Aspects. And he gained it from Urim. The Aspect of *all* knowledge. All that was required then was a willing vessel. Samyaza became that vessel, Mal'ak. Through Samyaza's body, Lucifer loosed the Blight upon the earth. Of course, Samyaza's freedom came at a terrible price. Unlike the Old Tongue, demon magic always carries a price," he said with a sniff. "But cost matters little to the damned, I suppose. Apparently, no price was too high to be free from Baal-Shadow."

"How did they do it?" asked Mal'ak.

"They did it at and through the moment of Eve's temptation, and Adam's weakness. With the fall of Adam and Eve, the dominion of earth was weakened. Lucifer's Blight spread like a devouring plague, corrupting not only the first man and woman, but the entire world succumbed to its touch. All was going according to plan, and Samyaza dared not hesitate. This would be his one and only chance to escape the realm of Baal-Shadow. Desperate to be free, he foolishly gave over his own essence, offering himself to the ravenous hunger of the Blight. Samyaza's screams echoed the halls of Baal-Shadow that night, and over time, became the only real constant to let him know that he still existed beyond the blinding pain of the curse that was gradually devouring him alive. Eventually, all traces of what he used to be were cankered away by the nameless evil he was becoming. Reality trembled at his coming—Lucifer at long last had created something of his own—Death! The mighty Seraph once known as Samyaza crawled forth from the depths of Baal-Shadow, as hell's firstborn. He *was* the Blight now, and much more. An avatar of a new kind, he was Death that lived, the only being in existence with rights to claim separation from God. Through Samyaza, Lucifer had created an abomination—an alternate reality apart from life—Life, which is the very nature of the Great Lord, Mal'ak—that part of God which of necessity occupies all of existence."

A lump formed in Mal'ak's throat as the images flashed before him, some so violent he wished he could avert his eyes, but he wasn't using his eyes, he was using the link.

"Lucifer and Samyaza invaded the reality of life like two hungry wolves and staked their claim, and what they claimed was precious, without price or measure." The Chronicler's voice quivered, but he continued. "They took from the Great Lord the souls of His own children, stole from them eternity. And man, which was created immortal, became mortal, and flesh began to die. The Fifth Age of Death had begun, and as my eyes burn, we stood powerless

188

to stop it. They are dying Mal'ak—all of them. All flesh born are infected with the Blight now, and to this cursed day, we have never found a cure. The Death demon's power over Adam's seed is undisputed. He has never been defeated in combat by the High-Bourne. By my recollections, Samyaza has never even been challenged—yet. Not even by Lucifer."

CHAPTER 11: LUCIFER AND THE DAWN

Lucifer took measure of the backwater town and snorted irritably. For the most part, it was a nothing little town with nothing important going on. The humans milling through the streets were poor and pathetic. A collection of farmers, merchants, and a few peddlers whose wares were priced higher than they were worth, but just a shade below the merchant's prices down the street. His scouts had reported a few shepherds coming in from the hill country to replenish waning supplies, but almost all of them had left town by midday, making the long trek back to their flocks. Most of the townsfolk were indoors and had no idea that hell itself sat at their doorstep. Demons large enough to swallow horses were roaming their streets and, as always, they were oblivious. Flesh-Walkers were the least of his worries, though. The bulk of Lucifer's forces had camped a stone's throw just south of the dirt street village. It would not have been his first choice for a campaign, and certainly not the best vantage point to engage the enemy. *But that's what happens when you get dumped out of a giant hole in the sky,* he thought ruefully. Shadows silently fingered their shade east, across the outskirts of town. It was still hours before dusk, but the sun hung low in the west, a molten ball of golden flame in a cherry sky. He scanned the horizon just like he had all evening, looking for traces of the quintessential fifth element, for all the good it did. They had been camped here for days now and still it proved as elusive as a shadow by moonlight.

"The Quintessenccce," he grunted. A sardonic smile twisted his mouth in a cool, sordid sneer. Experience told him the High-Bourne weapon could be hiding anywhere. There were only a thousand cubits that separated him from the High-Bourne tribes—not *nearly* far enough as far as he was concerned. Was it there? Hidden in the distance? Maybe it was the High-Bourne themselves—the actual number that were camped north? Sheol's flames, he knew it was hiding somewhere. It *was* in the numbers—it had to be. But which ones? The problem was the calculations themselves. There were too many, even for concurrent thought. He wrung his hands impatiently. The most logical place to look would be in the possibilities of outright war. For days he had been calculating the probable outcomes of battles played out on the field of his own mind, wrestling with the complex equations of warfare with the precision of a superlative intellect, and, of course, sorting out the timeliest means of escape—just in case. Satisfied with his efforts, the tension in his jaw relaxed, but only a little. "Light take my eyesss, I will not abide the Quintessenccce. *Anything* but that," he half muttered. Besides, the feel was off, or maybe

193

distant? Yes . . . distant was what his gut told him. *At least the earth has not swallowed us whole yet, or the Legion burst into spontaneous flames, or some other unexplainable ruin loosed upon us.* He grimaced. Those moments he knew all too well, and *this* particular moment was missing that hint of expectation, the kind that only happens before a miracle. *Sheol's flames,* he hated that word almost as fervently as he hated the Quintessence itself. There was not a hairs difference between the two, if that, and his campaigns against the High-Bourne with the Quintessence present had proven dismal at best. Something was not right about this night though, Quintessence or no, of that Lucifer was sure. And Light burn him, it started with the fact that no one was paying him proper fealty. Lucifer snorted at the flagrant lack of respect. Disputes among the Legion had ceased and that was odd enough all by itself. But why under the Light would hell and heaven stand silent together? While part of his brain scanned for the Quintessence, another part sifted through a thousand different scenarios of war, which only left the small corners of his mind to concentrate on simply shining. He had appeared as an angel of light earlier. He thought it was amusing. Currently, he outshone most of the celestial host—most of the lower caste, anyway. He was gunning for the higher caste, though. But then again, he might just settle for being *acknowledged* by his own kind at the moment. A salute, a bow . . . *something.* He pushed harder. Wide arcing bands of light exploded from his eyes, face and every pore. He was a kaleidoscope of colors, bathing anyone near in his radiance, and *still* no one noticed or seemed to care. Lucifer took umbrage at such brazen disrespect. *I—the Ssson of the Morning, ignored? The prince and power of the air cast assside like some whelp?*

"Have they forgotten who their lord isss?" he chewed the words through gritted teeth. A savage growl rumbled in the demon lord's throat, his façade as an angel of light wavering for an instant. Inhaling deeply, Lucifer rose to his full height when a shadow caught his attention from the corner of his eye. Something large and dark crept up behind him. *I'm being challenged? This is insanity*, he thought. Though Lucifer never turned his head, the dark figure was close enough to make out its shape. Lucifer swore under his breath. A foul creature of shadow was this ravenous beast that stalked him—a Mawgore hell demon that thrived on the fears of others and who had enough power to rival most any hell demon in the Legion ranks. Lucifer knew the creature well and had used his ilk on countless campaigns in ages past. Always to undermine, sometimes even paralyze the Great Lord's work on earth. The Mawgore traveled in packs like wolves, which was one of many reasons they were so feared, even by other Legion. Lucifer knew there were sure to be more of the beasts just out of sight, biding their time for the right moment to pounce. Their appetite for fear was insatiable. They nearly couldn't help themselves, a fact made clear by the way the Fear Beast so brazenly challenged him out in the open like this.

However, Lucifer *was* puzzled. He was not afraid of one Fear Beast or of the five or more waiting in the wings to pounce on him. *If their numbers were truly great, that might pose a problem,* he thought apprehensively. But that would be highly doubtful, given that the Mawgore were, well . . . Mawgore. They were dangerous to be sure, but brutish beasts with diminished intellect, and barely broken speech at that. On the other hand, the one thing he could not accuse the Mawgore of was outright stupidity. For what they lacked in intelligence they more than made up for in sheer brute strength and savage cunning. *Why would a Mawgore needlessly throw its own existence away by challenging me?* Lucifer pulled nervously at his chin as he turned the question around in his head. Fear attracted these demons like rotting carrion attracts maggots. When Lucifer spun his head around, he was startled to see it crouched so closely behind him. How it had made it this close without making a sound, he could only wonder. Two yellow orbs gazed at Lucifer, more primal than intelligent. Its body sat completely still while its skin crawled with something underneath. A thin membrane, gorged with liquid, blood red, rippled across the demon's hide. A smile touched Lucifer's lips, knowing it wasn't blood, but terror flowing underneath the demons skin. The beast was swollen almost to bursting with the fears of the Great Lord's children. It was empowered by their fear. It gave Lucifer pleasure. O yes, an appetite like this was rare even amongst Legion. The Mawgore could hound a child of the flesh tirelessly, even to the brink of despair, then feast on it while still alive. But its beauty lay in the harvest, how it could harvest the torments of its victims, trapping their fear to feast on later in a putrid sepulcher stored under its own skin. It literally wore their fears like a garment. Lucifer had dealt with these beasts before, and whether he enjoyed their feeding habits or not, he would end this quickly.

"Ssso be it, you fool of a demon," he hissed. Lucifer turned his entire body around to face the brash demon only a quarter his size.

Then he felt it. He had been so caught up in himself, in grand appearances. Somehow, he had missed it before. But he felt it *now*. The air was thick with it. It was holiness—the unmistakable, unapproachable holiness of the Great Lord himself. Lucifer's knees buckled and his legs went wobbly like untempered springs. He knew full well what was coming next. The calm shattered and fear began to run rampant through the ranks. The Fallen Legion were panicking.

They knew it was coming. The situation was quickly deteriorating, and yet clearer with each passing moment. At least he knew why no one had noticed him earlier, and why the Mawgore was emboldened to challenge him so. The beast's mind was not the most suitable home for sanity, but it would never challenge Lucifer under normal circumstances. The demon's skin was taut, bulging with the fear of the saints, but with the surrounding panic, so ripe with the fears of so many of his brethren, it must have overwhelmed the creature to the point of madness. *Sheol's flames, the fool beast was not challenging me at all,* he thought. It was just desperate to *stop* feeding—desperate to stop cannibalizing the terror of his own kind. It screamed, high pitch, like a woman insane, but higher, piercing the thick red atmosphere of the spirit realm with agony. Its howls reached above the chaos, touching the distant ears of the High-Bourne tribes across the divide. Its oversized mouth hung wide open, squealing, as essence bled through rows of yellow fangs. It panted in labored breaths, begging in a broken tongue for Lucifer to make an end of it. The translucent hide on its back began to tear, ripping under the strain of intense pressure, oozing a pungent liquid already coagulating on the ground, thick with the smell of rot and sulfur. The Mawgore's eyes bulged in its head as the gluttonous beast swelled three times its normal girth. Lucifer watched in macabre fascination as the demon groped its own head and body with clawed fingers, futilely trying to hold in the life giving fluid seeping out of its body, yet still feeding greedily, absorbing the very fears that were killing it.

A sense of dread filled Lucifer. Not for the Mawgore; he cared for the beast no more than he did an inanimate stone. Baal-Shadow would claim this one. Besides, Lucifer knew there were plenty more Mawgore. They were numerous in the Fallen Legion. No, the terror growing inside of him came from a singular compunction: he knew it was coming!

By the Silver Cord, how could this be happening? he thought, trying to stifle the fear bubbling up in his middle. Lucifer wheeled around, screaming at Samyaza, "The Dawn comes for usss!"

But the Death demon had already slunk back to the depths of Baal-Shadow. It wanted no part of what transpired here, no—it could *not be* a part of what transpired here. But then, how could *Death* stay in the presence of the Life Giver? Lucifer groaned.

He knew it was coming. Trying not to panic, he replayed the events as he recalled them earlier that evening. This was to be an unveiling, this ... Epoch Horizon, Lucifer almost spat the name in open disgust. "Dawn burn me, that was all. I never thought *He* would actually draw nigh."

Lucifer knew it was coming. It was more than just His holiness, although that alone was enough to send any demon scurrying for cover. Holiness was merely the hallowing evidence to His nearness. There was much, much more to Him than *that*. It was *He Who Brings the Dawn*, that Lucifer feared, the Great Lord himself, and He brought with Him Light. Light unlike any other, a cleansing dawn that pierced soul and spirit. It was this Light that sundered the darkness and quickened the world; it was the original. All others fall pitifully short when next to the nimbus of the King of all Kings. Lucifer braced himself. His eyes tightened as the brightness of a billion glimmering stars winked a single flicker then vanished from his view, awash in the Great Lord's divine aura. He shrieked as planet sized shafts of light shot forth from the ether, penetrating, seeking out shadow, exposing the dark regions of soul and spirit.

Lucifer knew full well that this light would not abide evil's presence. He knew that what it did not change, it burned—burned until it had purged the darkness from its presence. It was akin to everything inherent in the Almighty. It was eternal and its finality inescapable. Lucifer could only stand there, engulfed in holiness, mouth agape, watching, while the Light of the Great Lord wildly pursued its path toward an endless majesty, to herald the greatness of a glory with no end, and whose beacon shone ever brighter and brighter eternally. There was but one word to describe it all: GOD. He knew it. The angels *definitely* knew it. The High-Bourne basked in the brightness of God's great light. The eastern horizon held the glow of a billion wings extended, all of them aglow in reflective glory of their King.

For the Legion, however, it was pandemonium. Running this way and that, they clamored and clawed over one another, trying to find some crevice or hole to hide themselves. Many huddled behind him, behind Lucifer's bulk, hoping to find some reprieve from the luminous onslaught of the Dawn Bringer's nimbus. It pained Lucifer terribly, like the fires of Imrah touching his body; it burned hot and cutting. His facade as an angel of light was gone, engulfed by a presence much greater than his. Like a drop that dissolves in the ocean, it washed over him, stripping away the lie, revealing his true form: a great, red, scaled brute—a Dragon.

Mal'ak watched from the relative safety of the High-Bourne front lines. The Dawn's truth be told, he was enjoying every second of this moment and would be lying if he said any different. Quill and parchment had mysteriously found their way back into his hands again. The quill scribbled furiously across the page, capturing any detail he found significant, and some that he would later have to defend to the Chronicler. *Ta'ow are not overly curious,* Mal'ak thought, ears twitching. He was just . . . attentive to detail—that was all. Besides, today was among the rarest of occasions. He could not remember a time when he stood any closer to a Dragon lord. Well, there was Tannin, but he was of the gold. Lucifer was of the red Dragonkin, and that was totally different, he sniffed. *Somebody needs to journal this out,* thought Mal'ak. *A proper theorem of Dragonkin anatomy could be useful.* "Anything less is just bad journaling, sighed Mal'ak," dabbing the nib of his quill in his inkwell. Mal'ak rested his eyes on Lucifer, letting the numbers fall along the contours of the arch demon's body. Lucifer's wings loomed large, by the lines, thirty cubits from wing-tip to wing-tip, easily dwarfing all but the highest ranks among the Legion. He was a patchwork of armor in diamond shaped scales with no weakness, at least none that could be determined by the High-Bourne. Though in his training, the General had theorized that the smaller scales adorning the demon's underbelly and wings *might* be susceptible to attack from underneath. Mal'ak grinned. Lucifer did seem to be standing exactly how the General said he would be, at least while grounded. His wings were folded tightly against his back. But susceptible to attack? Mal'ak shook his head. No one else but the General would pick up on something like that, or dare try, for that matter. Dawn's Light, Mal'ak could probably count on one hand the number of angels willing to put *that* theory to the test, although he was absolutely positive that at some point the General would personally test its validity.

Lucifer was obviously in pain. He shook visibly, his head swinging from side to side while more and more demons crowded in behind him. Not since before the Age of the Turning had Mal'ak seen the Dragon lord's face, and never in his fallen state. The fall had not been kind to the elder demon.

Black eyes as hard as stone roamed the short distance of meadow separating them. Earlier, Lucifer had openly strode through the ranks of his own army, the epitome of confidence. Now, he was in agony. Mal'ak could see it marked all over the ancient demon's face, not to mention, his red hide sizzled like meat being cooked. Mal'ak wondered at how much more the Dragon lord could take. His movements were labored, *probably because of the pain*, thought Mal'ak. Still, his movements felt almost feline, even through the pain of the Great Lord's nimbus bearing down on him. 'A Dragon lord moves without reticence...' Mal'ak journaled, his tufted ears a flutter, eyes darting up and down, his quill a scrawling blur across the parchment as he continued his appraisal. *Dragons come in different sizes.* In truth, there was not much of a size difference between the reds and golds like Tannin. But to a Crafter's eye, it was notable, so he recorded it. *Both are enormous, and both have huge, oversized jaws. Lucifer in particular has a mouth full of black fangs. Some look to be as long as a Ta'ow's arm length.* This gave Mal'ak the shivers, but he scrawled on. *Set within Lucifer's brow are ten black horns, dark as polished onyx. Nine protruding from the top of his skull and one bearding the end of his chin. One horn in particular is shorter than the rest. Broken, it stands roughly half the size of the others, the shaft's end jagged with sharp crystalline edges. In the horn's center is a soft spongy marrow. It secrets black fluid, tinged with green swirls on the end of the jagged nub. It seems to ooze freely.* The best Mal'ak could tell, it oozed essence, and quite a bit at that. It wetted the cracks that splintered the damaged horn, mixing with the taint of shadow magic. It was said the wound would never heal, but served as a bitter reminder of the one who tore it asunder— the one who ripped the horn from his brow in the Age of the Turning. It was the General who told Mal'ak this story, and laughed in the telling of it, saying, "Lucifer *never* speaks of this. He acts as if it never happened." He also told Mal'ak that the ebon horns upon Lucifer's head were mystical in nature and deadly. Inside them, a vile darkness dwelled, lethal to the world. Lucifer was a lord of Baal-Shadow with the power to bind shadow—to bend the darkness to his will and traverse its corridors wherever shadow exists. By the High-Bourne's own estimation, binding shadow was a rare gift, even among the higher ranks of the Legion. The High-Bourne theorized that the dark gift was accorded to Lucifer by the Death lord, Samyaza. Mal'ak figured it was by this same power that Samyaza had fled the realm of earth at the Great Lord's appearing. Baal-Shadow . . . a place of living shadows, where the Grigori dwell, and angels fear to tread. Mal'ak shivered again. The dark realm lay hidden, somewhere between the realms of spirit and earth. The one place even Ta'ow curiosity did not want to see. It could stay hidden, and Samyaza with it, as far as Mal'ak was concerned.

He was puzzled, though. Why *had* Lucifer stayed? What on earth would possess the Dragon lord to try and stand before the Great Lord's nimbus? It was madness.

Careless, thought Lucifer, cursing himself for a fool. *I should never have come here.* He knew his own pride was to blame, but the allure of gloating before the High-Bourne tribes and the entire kingdom of heaven proved too great a temptation to resist. *If not for the nimbusss . . .* He stifled a groan. That infernal Light not only burned his scales, it also burned away the darkness—*all* of it. Not a single trace of shadow was left to steal away or make good his escape. He was trapped. His mind searched frantically for an obscure augury he might have overlooked, a sign he might have missed, but there was nothing. *Nothing.* He was sure of it. *Will God kill me now?* he thought. *Sheol's flames—like this? And what of the prophecies? The Messiah has not yet entered the realm of flesh. I would have known, surely.* His mind was a jumble of prophecies mixed with partially answered questions. *By the Sssilver Cord,* he ground his teeth, "He won't take me now.

The Great Lord can never break his own word," the words dripped from Lucifer's mouth with open scorn. "It is not my time," he said to himself. "Is it?"

Nothing made sense anymore. He wanted to flee, but neither the light nor pride would let him. His mouth was dry and he struggled to focus. Completing a thought was an effort at this point. He could feel his scales beginning to soften. They were melting. Sheol's flames, he wanted to fall on his face and beg for mercy, but in front of so many, how could he? The Legion were done. They baked in God's nimbus while begging for mercy. And the truth of it was, he was done too. He could not even manage to stand in the Dawn Bringer's presence–not like this, not in full glory; nothing could. Nothing that was fallen. His tongue trembled with a thousand pleas for mercy. He opened his mouth and suddenly, it all stopped.

CHAPTER 12: A BABY?

Strangely, the light of the Great Lord departed as suddenly as it had come. The air was still, and night reclaimed its silence. Lucifer's scales whistled a high sizzling noise as smoke climbed high in the air, bringing with it the stench of cooked demon hide. Not just his, but all in the Legion. In the quiet, Lucifer found himself face down on the ground, handfuls of dirt filling his taloned fists. Slowly he unclenched, taking in his surroundings once again. He shook himself, trying to shake off the grogginess, but his head was still reeling from the onslaught. "By the

Sssilver Cord, I'm still here," he muttered. "He spared me." Instantly, his relief was replaced by unbridled rage. Hatred boiled hot inside him. He would not be seen cowering in weakness–never weakness. Gathering himself, he clenched his jaws, and with a deep breath, stood straight up. Pride swelled his chest and his posture was pure defiance, but when he opened his eyes, breath and hubris drained right out of him. Except for the occasional whimper, demon and angel joined him in awkward silence. No one spoke.

For a moment it seemed that time itself stood still . . . or started over again, he wasn't quite sure which. Lucifer had seen extraordinary things in his long life. He had heard the power-wrought canticles of angels in the Old Tongue, and had lived in Heaven for what would seem like an eternity to a mortal man. He had even attended the throne of God. But nothing in the heavenly city or on earth could have prepared him for this. Wide mouthed astonishment held him there. He could not move, only stare.

Every eye in the realm of spirit this night rested upon

one small girl in a dirt-nothing town called Bethlehem. Her name was Mary. A brown-eyed Jewish girl, maybe fourteen earth years of age. She had just given birth, her face, tear streaked from the pains of labor, but smiling like she knew something that the world did not. And the numinous light that illuminated the darkness of the realms and had shaken Lucifer to his knees was merely a small glow nestled in young Mary's arms.

"By the Sssilver Cord! Closer," he said, thoughts that were not thoughts anymore but spoken aloud. "Must get . . . *clossser.*" Lucifer's eyes worked fine at this distance, but his mind would not accept what was right in front of him. He approached, cautiously at first.

It was brown-eyed and dimple cheeked, with little rolls of fat around its tiny hands and feet. It had ten fingers, ten toes, two eyes and a mouth full of drool. Sheol's flames. It was just . . . a baby?

"Impossible!" he spat. Hell fire plumed orange flickering hot from his snout, scorching the ground where he stood. Of course, Bethlehem carried on, oblivious to the danger, as if nothing in the world were amiss. Crickets competed in the wood-line for the night's loudest song while the animals in the stables settled in. Mary had swaddled her baby in a rag, setting him, of all places, in a feeding trough. Her husband lay asleep while she lay awake, softly humming and caressing her baby's cheek with her hand. *That* was when Lucifer saw it. The first sign. Mary was young. She was just a girl. But still she was contaminated with the Blight, a Flesh-Walker. Even at this tender age, her hand was already withering. Lucifer could see the skin aging—her body slowly dying. That *is* what the Blight does—it kills flesh. But the Child, he noticed, was *completely* clean—pure, *immortal*. Somehow, the Blight did not touch it. Lucifer's eyes narrowed. Throwing caution to the wind, he pushed his way in, wading through his forces like barley in a field, quickly closing the distance between himself and the child. The light of the Great Lord had departed this realm; of *that* much he was sure. Shadow had recovered patches of ground in the nooks of trees and ringed the bottom of rocks scattered along the red colored clay of the Spirit realm. *At least the shadow had returned*, he thought. Something was different though–an echo remained. Not so much an echo, but the whisper of an echo. He inhaled and his spine tingled, his nostrils flared, confirming what countless millennia had taught him. Holiness still remained . . . not here, but close. He snorted a great stream of smoke, exhaling the stench from his snout. *No, not here*, he thought. *But in the realm of flesh*. He could sense its presence much like the human sense of smell, only more keen, depending upon the source. And the source of this holiness was unmistakable . . . that sickening sweet smell of nectar and wild clover made his stomach want to empty right there. And it was emanating entirely from Mary's baby.

Lucifer growled his deep rumbling disgust, loud and unrestrained. His horns glowed red hot, haloed by a greenish glow at their tips as he invoked the power of shadow to aid him. The shadows began to whisper and come forth with life of their own. Opaque tendrils, black like oil, slithered from the depths. They entwined his legs, crawling their way slowly up his torso toward his head. There he stood, a murky clot of shadow. The only hint of a Dragon remaining was the spiked tip of his tail twitching nervously from side to side, his head, and the horned tip of his wings piercing the black veil. He was standing a mere five hundred and ninety-four cubits from Mary and her babe, dangerously close to an almost countless number of High-Bourne. Lucifer's momentary lapse in judgment left him vulnerable at best, even cloaked in shadow, for one whose eyes burned with the heat of a sun gazed fiercely upon him, eyes that burned as hot with hatred for the elder demon as they did with flame. Of course Lucifer knew the danger. It wasn't that he didn't care, he was simply too caught up in the child to bother with concern. Besides, this vantage point suited his needs much better. From here he peered into the child's body, underneath its skin, searching desperately for one thing.

"Where iss it?" he hissed under his breath. His eyes

CHAPTER 12: A BABY?

shifted from side to side, hunting, almost frantic for evidence of the divine origins he was sure that lay somewhere in that baby. As it was, the child made him nauseous. The scent of holiness hung sweet in the air like wild lilies mixed with honeysuckle in spring. It turned his stomach almost to vomiting and he was getting more nauseous by the second. "Where iss it?" He glowered. "The Dawn burn me, where is the ssseparation?" His gaze penetrated Mary's baby deeper and deeper, into muscle fibers and tissues, scanning for something, anything, that might be out of the ordinary. Carefully, he examined the organs. The baby's heart and lungs were tiny, but all was as it should have been. There was *nothing* that would seem out of order or extraordinary. Impatiently, his long tail flicked, and dark smoke leaked out from two protruding slits in his muzzle, leaving the scent of sulfur wafting on the air. His eyes moved on to the bones and marrow, then the brain. "Nothing," he murmured.

Exasperated, he searched deeper, smaller now, into white and red blood cells, sifting through arteries and veins, into tiny capillaries that spider webbed into the millions, where the child's blood raced hot with the vigor of newborn life. Lucifer searched on, deeper and deeper, and smaller still. Then, he froze. His back slowly unarched. His armored scales slid against one another, rustling like leaves against a snake's belly. As his eyes widened, they held an unfamiliar gleam of wonder. Lucifer had been searching for a separation. A seam, no matter how small, that would separate the child's divine essence from its flesh and humanity. But what he found was altogether different. Deep within the recesses of the child's body, he found the building blocks of humanity. And there, somewhere woven into the child's DNA was no mere spark or trace, but the makings of deity itself. There *was* no seam! The child *was* the Great Lord, and the child was man.

Lucifer's mind was pregnant with awe, swirling on the prospect of the Creator creating . . . himself?

"The *imago dei* . . . but how?"

The words had barely escaped his mouth before the answer barged in on his consciousness. God *never* asks how.

CHAPTER 12: A BABY?

Lucifer was amazed—he did not want to be, but he was. He could not stop looking at it, nor could he seem to stretch his intellect far enough to wrap around it. He was impressed. A moment like this could not be denied, even by him. It was a moment for the ages. The *imago dei*, the image of God is a woman-birthed Flesh-Walker? *Flesh*, he thought. *The Blight has infested that stuff.*

"I personally made sure of that." He sneered, a half smile that creased his lips. He could think of no greater demotion than this. Sheol's flames, even *he* could think of no greater... Love. The word caught awkwardly in his throat, and jealousy flooded the dark hollows of his heart. He no longer knew or even remembered what it was to love, to feel the exhilaration of its embrace, or the pain of its loss. To Lucifer, God's greatest gift—Love—was dead. His heart was stone, seared with hate. Inside him was a darkness unimaginable, where things such as remorse or guilt no longer existed. He was a bottomless well of hate with an insatiable hunger to torment flesh—*especially* the Dawn Bringer's children. This filled him with pleasure and something that might be akin to joy—if he could've still felt joy. But now, hate filled him, filled him with rage at a Flesh-Walker favored like this. The *imago dei*—the image of the Great Lord himself—born of flesh.

Lucifer's eyes glazed, narrowing to slits. He reared his broad head, sucked in a gulp of air and roared violently, laying curses upon the babe, screaming blasphemies at the child, while sulfurous pillars of smoke billowed from his gaping maw. Hell fire leaped wildly from his nostrils, until the child stirred. When he did, Lucifer's mouth snapped shut in a hard line as hell and all of her armies fell back a full step, cowering before the child . . . a God child! Sword and armor clashed against pole-arm as war mounts danced nervously. Their roars and impish squeals rumbled across the hard red clay like a thunderclap, rattling Lucifer's bones with their fear of the child. For long moments it rolled.

The child's hand raised slowly into the air . . . and he yawned.

CHAPTER 13: THE GREAT SONG OF SONGS

Mal'ak's mouth fell slack, then a wide toothy grin slowly spread across his face as he looked at the Legion, at the baby, then to the Legion again. *They're afraid of Him*, he thought, biting his lip and trying not to laugh. *This might be the greatest humbling in history, and I was there to see it!* His ears fluttered with amusement. Oh, if only Adam could see this. Dragons afraid of a baby. Mal'ak snickered, cupping a hand over his mouth while trying to thumb the nib of his quill back to life with his other hand. His inkwell was near dry, but he should have just enough to record this. Oh yes . . . his quill would capture *every* detail of this moment.

****

Lucifer scowled. He had been cowed to silence along with everyone else. And what was worse? The Legion were watching. That cursed thing had not been in the world for more than a few moments and already he was brought low by the child's simple gesture.

Then without warning, a crackle like lightning assaulted his ears and the world hazed to a blur. His hold over the shadow wavered, flickering in and out of darkness, and a cold that burned like the fires of Imrah washed over him.

"Sheol's flames," he managed through gritted teeth. A sickening ball bubbled in his middle. He had been burned like this before. He *knew* power. And power like this could only be wrought from the God Flow, the mystery of primal life coalesced into pure flame–the flame that was not a flame. Not really. Even a whelp new to the shadow knew that. Of course he was *there* when the creation spark was breathed into man, and the sons of clay awoke to life, sealed to the flame. It was this same torrential flow that spun the galaxies and binds creation to exist, that bound he himself to existence. The thought skittered across his consciousness like water dashed on a hot stone. With effort, he stuffed the thought away.

Lucifer could have *sworn* he heard singing, like a soft melody whispering on the breeze. But then the voice was gone. Or was it really there to begin with? Sheol's flames, he was unaccustomed to diffidence. His thoughts were slippery, and any resolve he could muster felt as shaky as his legs. Everything felt . . . *off.* More like a dream than the waking world.

****

Lucifer perched atop the highest peak of the highest mountain. The garden of God spread before him in grandeur. Only the white spires of the Great Lord's Kingdom could hope to eclipse Eden's beauty. The morning sun was half a cherry drop draped in tangerine sky. The briny tang of sea blew in from the north shore, stirring his hair, whistling through the crags of the canyons to the valley below. A song rose on the wind, a familiar voice, strong and beautiful. By the Dawn, it was beautiful, and close. *Wait . . . that voice . . . it sounds like my voice? It is my voice. I'm singing!* His skin pebbled as the chorus of an ancient melody boomed from his own throat. It was the Old Tongue, and his chest ached with the memory of it. The Song of Songs, it was called. He remembered. He remembered how to sing. He remembered it *all!*

Looking down at his hands, he gasped. His scales were gone. He was a Cherub again. He was undiminished. By the Dawn, he was the Daystar. The morning air frosted his breath, and his body heaved like a bellows. Horns extended from his sides, blowing, filling the air with the crescendos of a living instrument, and he was just getting started. Covered in precious stones, he stood, marveling at his own image. Beryl flanked his sides, and scarlet clusters of rubies and sardius stone plated his chest, both accented with onyx as dark as starless night around the edges. His hands stroked fondly at his throat, sleek and overlaid in diamonds, while his back and wings glittered of sapphires and topaz in the morning light.

He spread his wings like a phoenix, a son of fire, born in a sunrise. He was the Son of the Morning, made by the Great Lord himself, fashioned from the full pattern of wisdom's storehouse and beauty's lavish grace. He had no equal among the heavens, and was surpassed by only one . . . his Creator.

This could not be, and he knew it, but reason had given over to the call of the Song. The Great Song was all that mattered. It was everything. Everything he remembered, and more, except the words were missing, the names were missing. But that was normal. The names were wrought in

229

power and could not be uttered without the crooning of the ancient melody to bring them about. But *oh*, how he crooned. *Soon*, he thought, licking his lips eagerly.

Power flooded him. The flow of the pattern filled his limbs and he held on for dear life. For *life* is exactly what he held on to—as much as you could hold on to a river and not be swept away. A sapphire flood channeled through him, more than enough to hull him out if he drew in too much. His body was a conduit now, a channel for the Great Song of Songs, and his mouth the sluice gate. The greatest force in creation pushed through him, the language of God unlocked in a melody. Voices began to rise from the valleys below.

A smile pulled at the corners of Lucifer's mouth. He had not even called their names yet, and already creation was singing the Dawn Bringer's glory.

"I hear you," he said, his voice echoing down the slopes through the canyons below. "I can hear you all!"

Behind him, in the east meadow, the firmament was dappling dew upon mountain lilies nestled in the cliffs. The lilies in turn swayed in the breeze launching the dew into the springs below with a rain song.

"Perfect," he cheered. Water and air were the first two names that appeared on his tongue. Deftly he plucked the *patter patter* of rain song out of the air, then looped the sound in an array of spheres woven from air. He held the spheres aloft, catching the morning light of the sun at just the right angle and a rainbow appeared across the breadth of the canyon. He smiled, opening his mouth wider, drawing in more of the flow. Spirit joined air and water. The three raced through him. Their names and many others formed on his tongue as he crooned the Creator's song. Turning his head north, he set his gaze upon the Deep and called forth the Song of the Tides. The waters answered their name with a swell that crashed against the cliffs like thunder. Water shot up the sheer face to the peaks above, even higher than where Lucifer stood. He laughed as wave upon wave pounded against the northern face of Eden. "Sing!" he said, cheering them on. Elms and Cedars clapped their branches with the *knock knock* of wood, their leaves swooshing through the air like the sizzle of cymbals, their voices a sonorous rumble felt more than heard.

Lucifer spun and danced, drawing the names in intricate rune patterns, singing the names of creation into the air with his voice and hands. The spheres he had woven of air captured the sound without diminishing frequency or vibration, so he could build the harmony structure, voice upon voice with a near infinite number of sounds to choose from and then release them back into the atmosphere in staggering power. The Song's power was absolute, and with it he built a choir ten million voices strong and counting. Their chorus shook the mountain beneath his feet. No song had ever been orchestrated like this before, and he knew it, but he desired more. He was full to the brim with the pattern, and still his heart ached for *more* of the God-Flow. He shuddered as the sweet rage of sapphire flame rocketed through him. Already, it threatened to turn him to cinder where he stood. It was folly to draw in more, but he would not let it go . . . not yet.

He set his gaze to the stars. Only the heavens stood silent before him now—only the stars. *Is this folly?* His head was spinning. He'd already held the power too long. He should release it all. But why?

He stood above them all, did he not? Was not this a *form* of glory as well? Was not *he* in the right to partake of a glory orchestrated by his own hand? He stared up at the stars. Even above the din that shook the mountain, he could hear them. The planets hummed and the stars roared flames of power unimaginable. He drew breath and opened himself—*all* of himself this time.

And the God-Flow rushed into every crevice. By the Dawn, he felt alive. Maybe more alive than he'd ever felt before. With *this*, he held true power. He *was* power. With this, creation unveiled herself to him. Naked, she whispered her names to his ear. With this, he would ascend and make his throne *above* the stars, in the uttermost parts of the north.

There is no council that can hide from me now, he

thought, wide eyed, drunk on more power than he'd ever dreamed possible. Tears outlined the rims of his eyes, his body twisted from the strain, but he didn't care. He took up an oath. "Dominion is mine. The Song is mine. And with it I will serenade the stars to dance before *me*. I will make myself like the Most High, and all thrones shall bow before the Daystar."

The God-Flow rocketed through him, through the pattern of the melody, almost too fast for him to see which flows were which. Air, water, spirit, light, and fire and flows born of creation he'd never seen before raced through him.

"I will guide them all," he howled. "I know *your* names too," he shouted to the stars. The heavens shuddered. The stars and planets slowly turned in their orbit, starring down at him.

"Yes," he shouted. "The Daystar calls to you."

Creation screamed. The seas rose up and fled, and the earth cracked beneath his feet. A third of the stars fell before him. Some fled inward, extinguishing their flame within the void of a black hole. Others fell from the heavens in silence, burning the sky in their despair, and Lucifer sang on.

Horrified, creation tried to resist him, but was helpless against the Song's power. The sky was riven and the heavens moaned. Lucifer violated them, forcing his will upon them. He used them for his own passion and they knew it, using *their* voice for another glory. *His* glory. The Elms and Cedars of the forest cried out, the Olive groves fled to the east, and the mighty Oaks struck at the base of the mountain, but it was useless. They were defenseless against his advances. And he was not going to stop. In one final attempt to stop him, the trees of Eden came up with a plan. They grew their mouths shut—forever sealing their voices, rather than give their song to another. Stilling their branches, they burrowed deep, rooting themselves in the rich clay of Eden's soil, never to walk or talk again. Tears . . . the first ever cried, rolled down Lucifer's cheeks.

"You would rather diminish yourselves than sing to me?" he asked in shock. "You would rather have no face at *all* than to look at *me?* Am I not a good God? Do you not see? If you would just sing . . . to *me.*"

The air about him churned with an aura that seemed to eat away the light of day. And there, on the mountain of God itself, his heart turned. Love drained out of him like it had been poured through a sieve, and in its absence, something else flourished. He felt cold and numb. Hate narrowed his eyes to slits.

"You *will* sing to me. I will make you!" he screamed. He called the Song of the Winds, commanding the wind to animate their lifeless limbs. But rooted to the ground as they were, they swayed back and forth, groaning, flailing in the wind, no voice, no song. Their limbs he controlled, but there was no consciousness left in them. Their hearts were as cold and hard as the wood of their skin.

Lucifer staggered back. He had held onto the Song too long. His mouth ached with the strain of keeping it open and his teeth felt as though they were loosing from their sockets. Desperately, he strained to hold the flows, but he wasn't holding the flows anymore . . . the flows were holding him.

"No!" he screamed, as a sliver of memory stabbed at his chest. "Not again. I will not abide this again. Please!" The God-Flow forced his mouth open wider, burning him alive from the inside out, and creation burned with him.

"Pleassse, not again," he begged. He was changing, just like before, and like before, creation was changing with him. Scales formed on his hands and his mouth morphed into a reptilian snout. He did not know which was worse, the changing, the burning, or reliving the memory of it all. The Song was lost to him. The flow no longer made sense anymore. The melody was distorted, ugly, and he was its reflection. The more the flow twisted inside him, the more twisted his body became. "Mercccy," he cried. "Mercccy!"

Suddenly, he was back. Bethlehem was the Haze as it had been before. He wrung his hands, trying to stop them from shaking. He didn't even have to look down. The length of his claws and the plated scales of a reptile's hands told him . . . he was a Dragon again. Sadness filled him and he

237

shoved it back with a sniff. *A dream?* he wondered uneasily. Sheol's flames, it felt so real. So clear, so . . . .

He stopped, cursing himself for a fool.

"The Chronicler," he spat. The obvious disdain for the name gave Lucifer's voice a bladed edge. A soft melody floated on the breeze . . . Lucifer shook his head. "Concentrate, burn you." The attack was as ruthless as it was brilliant, and he was still trapped, half inside a dream song, dreaming of the Great Song of Songs. The irony left a bitter taste in his mouth and being maneuvered so easily galled him.

"For *that* you will bleed," he said, wiping saliva from his mouth. He knew the Chronicler well. The Word Smith was gifted in the Old Tongue . . . as Lucifer had been so painfully reminded. He knew few High-Bourne aside from Gabriel who could accomplish such a feat—especially against one such as himself. Over the millennia, rumors had circulated through the ranks of the Legion that Gabriel could enthrall a demon within a dream from which it might never awake, not until the High-Bourne's blade found its mark, anyway. It had even been said that Gabriel could touch the God-Flow through the Old Tongue.

Lucifer shuddered at such a thought. That was ludicrous. He believed less than half of what the Legion told him anyway. More than half of what they swore on oath were excuses to cover up ineptness. Lucifer sniffed contemptuously. If the Chronicler was aware that he was aware, nothing had changed. The melody played on, soft, barely audible on the breeze.

"A melody *indeed*," Lucifer sneered. He was not free yet, but he was ready this time. Still half in, and half out of the dream song, he reached out with his mind . . . reached for the Shadow—the one thing the Chronicler's song could not touch. Lucifer felt the telltale seep of his own essence bleeding down the length of his broken horn. He welcomed the sting, welcomed the sensation of demon shadow slithering around his body, cold and familiar. A half smile almost split his face. He narrowed his brow in concentration, drawing hard upon the arcane flows. He shivered, feeling it pulse over his skin again, racing icy cold through him. The Chronicler was strong, and it would take all of Lucifer's will to break free.

Using the shadow itself as an anchor, he began pulling himself bit by bit from the Chronicler's song. He giggled an insane laugh as he felt the last of the Chronicler's charms fade from him. At last, he was free...

CHAPTER 14:
THE GENERAL

Lucifer knew he had gotten careless. Preoccupation with the child had left him vulnerable, to say nothing of letting himself be lulled by the Chronicler's song. But where were they going with this? He had a sense of foreboding that he couldn't shake. A sense that he was being goaded. Why? Sheol's flames, and for what purpose? Summoning stones? The Narrows, the Epoch Horizon, and now this . . . *dream* song?

Why haven't the High-Bourne moved yet? Smoke puffed up, disappearing in thinning gray spirals that stretched from Lucifer's nostrils. He shifted uneasily. Again, he was uncertain, and he was *never* uncertain. At least his vision was returning, but what he saw caused him to question if he'd not been better off back inside the dream song. He found himself standing between a gap, already too small for his liking. By the Dawn, he had no idea how he had come this far. The High-Bourne stood before him—*all* of them— and their new born Sovereign. Behind him, hell looked on in open mouthed wonder. He was standing somewhere past the middle. Close, way too close to High-Bourne swords, spears and who knew what else, and he wasn't alone. As his eyes adjusted, his heart sank. He was not in the presence of the Chronicler at all, but a short distance from the blade of Imrah Light-Bringer, a sword of legend, forged in the halls of Heaven, tempered seven times within the fires of the great wheel of a Seraph's heart, with flames that could burn even a lord of Baal-Shadow. And the heat . . . .

"Dawn take me," he gasped. The heat emanating from it was immense. Blue flame danced from tip to hilt, crawling up the arms of its bearer, setting afire the shoulders and chest, licking the face of the one who wielded it. Through the azure blaze, Lucifer could make out runes bored deep into the flat of the blade. The runes inlaid upon Light-Bringer did not have the look of something fashioned with hands, nor did the blade itself. It looked more like a thing forged from light, with its broad, almost transparent blade spanning a full cubit in width, and its length that of a tall man. The vermeil guard above the hilt glistened in the shape of two wings on either side of the glowing shaft, while the hilt was gilded in narrow strips of Silver Weave accented with golden manna leaf, winding around to a pommel bearing the seal of the King of all Kings, a large golden Lion's head. Hilt and blade seemed to meld seamlessly into one another.

Lucifer's eyes widened. He found himself wishing it had been the Chronicler he was facing. He grimaced, recognizing the runes upon Light-Bringer as Old Tongue in written form. Lucifer had never seen so much of it at one time, not even before the Age of the Turning. Slowly, as astonishment wrestled with trepidation, he became keenly aware that he was looking upon the entire Word of God, *all* of the Old Tongue, canonized on the flats of that legendary blade. Light-Bringer hummed with power, droning a soft but steady cadence to the dance of the flame while the runes moved about the blade in a smooth hypnotic melody that drifted softly on the wind.

It was the blade, he thought in horror. *It was the blade the whole time.* He watched in disbelief as it shifted from praise to promise, from promise to Psalm, keeping rhythm with its blaze. It was alive.

Lucifer felt its eyeless stare looking right through him. He averted his eyes from the sword, only to meet the gaze of the one who wielded it. Even through the glare of the cobalt flames, Lucifer could see his face. Two yellow eyes, burning like twin suns stared back at him. It was Archistrategos—the General.

Lucifer sniffed, glancing away as casually as he could. He'd never seen a High-Bourne of such stature. The

CHAPTER 14: THE GENERAL

General was even larger than Lucifer remembered—huge by human standards.

The General crouched over the Holy child. His dark hair fell in crevices over thick muscled shoulders, shoulders easily spanning four cubits. He was blessed with the same ageless face of all High-Bourne, but his countenance carried a fierceness unmatched among his kind. To meet *his* gaze on the battlefield, for most, meant death. A gray tunic clung to his frame, a simple design from feather-cloth, with no seams and no sleeves. Lucifer could tell it was fashioned from the feathers of the archangel's own wings, as were the tunics of all the High-Bourne tribes. The color of his tunic matched the shaded hues of his wings perfectly and bore the symbol of the Eternal One's nimbus—an unbroken circle—Halo, surrounding a golden Lion's head.

Lucifer was wary of those wings. He had seen the General loose those feathered quills before. Like razored embers, they could cut through most any hell-spawn's defense with lethal effect. He was every demon's worst nightmare. His arms and hands had the look of burnished bronze, and in them was the raw strength to rip a demon in half, while his legs boasted the girth of two good oaks. It was he who held the blade, Imrah Light-Bringer, and it was the General and the High-Bourne tribes who had cast Lucifer from the heavens so long ago in the Age of the Turning. Lucifer knew he must tread carefully. He was not sure he could best the General in combat even under *normal* circumstances. The last time they met was *without* Imrah the Light-Bringer, and this was anything but *normal*.

Sheol's flames, this is the embrace of insanity, Lucifer thought. A flesh walking God Child? The *imago dei*, lying in a feed trough, with the God-Flow all over it. Who knew what the child could or would do? For that matter, who was to say whether Imrah wouldn't burn him to ash where he stood? The calculations in his head mounted fast, and he didn't like the odds. Too many uncertainties.

Well . . . he *was* sure about one thing. The General never backed down . . . ever. Unless the Great Lord told him

CHAPTER 14: THE GENERAL

to. *Blood and ashes,* he felt so off balance. Like a novice again. He rolled his eyes contemptuously. He was not sure the best course of action, or if he should take any action at all, but burn him if he was going to back down now. So, he sniffed the air, cocked his eyes side long, looking down arrogantly upon the angelic masses, and fell back on what he did best. He lied. But his lies were mingled with truths that flowed from his mouth like sweet manna mixed with honey. Lucifer, as non-threateningly as he could, arched his long neck and head to one side, still uncomfortable, even at this distance, with how close he stood to Light-Bringer's edge. The blade still hovered in the General's hands, directly over the child. Lucifer rose to his full height, wearing hubris like a second skin, and a sly smile slid across black teeth as long as a man's leg as he said, "Michael. Ah . . . faithful Michael. It has been a while, hasn't it? Or should I address you as Achistrategosss . . . or maybe . . . the General, is it? Is that what they call you in this age? My legionsss frequently return to me bearing the scars of your blade . . . *General.* Sometimesss they never return at all. Tell me, do you find pleasure in marking them? Branding demon skin with your own sword? Does it bring you humor . . . *General?* Blood and ashesss, and they call me cruel?" Lucifer chortled. "Come now, what are they to ones such as you and I anyway? Fodder? Would you not say the same? Surely nothing more. Are they not mere casualties to be used by the whims of thossse who are, and always will be, their superiors?

The General stood silent.

"No matter," Lucifer said smoothly. "Though there is one question I must ask you . . . *General.* Do you ever tire of serving the Great Lord? You must be utterly sick of it," he drawled. "Have you not had your fill? Serving millennia after millennia, age after age, still serving? Where has it gotten you, Michael? What hasss it made you? A general . . . who serves? Please! That doesn't even make sense. Do you never grow weary of being a glorified lap dog? I know, I know." He sighed. "The Prime Command." He chomped his teeth down, and sniffed. Cocking his head, he looked down the length of his nose. "I know exactly what you are thinking, Michael. 'I must preserve the Prime Command!'" The militant air in Lucifer's voice did little to hide the mockery of each word. "Tell me, Michael, what *is* the Great Lord's 'Prime Command?' Isn't it to preserve the human will? Their right to choossse? To protect and preserve at *any* cost their right to believe—their right to faith? *Faith?*" Lucifer stifled his laughter with one clawed hand. "Do you honestly believe there is any 'faith' left inside of these Flesh-Walkers? Do you? Do you see any Prophets proclaiming *the day of the Great Lord is at hand?* Hmm . . . I don't either.

"Oh yesss, and 'free will.' Their right to 'choose'?" He gurgled the words, lips trembling to keep back his amusement. "Mustn't forget that part. Tell me this, General. What do you *think* humans chose? Hmm . . . ? I'll tell you what they chose. They chose the Blight, Michael. They chose Death. You and your High-Bourne call humansss the true lords of this realm? Really? You actually believe that sons of clay could rule where sons of fire dwell?"

Lucifer sniffed, then squared his gaze on Michael. "They are exactly what I have made them to be and nothing more. They are fallen remnants of a broken trinity—forgotten children, infected with a disease that cannot be cured. General . . . I'm winning, and there is nothing you can do about it," he said through gritted teeth. "Do you know why? This is my favorite part," he whispered, his tone triumphant and thick with venom. "Are you ready for thisss? I will win because of the Great Lord's own Prime Command."

With that, Lucifer lost himself, the complete irony of it all coming out of him in a full bellied laugh. He didn't even bother to hide his contempt. "It was *their* choice," he said smugly "Free will, was it not? You see now, who rules this realm, Michael? It is I, the Son of the Morning, who bends the Great Lord's will to his own. God is weak, pathetic. Come now," he chided smoothly. "You are Archistrategosss, The Great Tacticianer. Surely you, above all other High-Bourne, can see the folly of thisss strategy? A God who cannot lie can be ensnared by His own Words. And a God that can be ensnared by His own Words is not worthy to rule. Think of the irony, Michael." Lucifer's eyes widened with pride as he boasted. "I am using the Great Lord's Prime Command, His very own immutable laws, to condemn His own children to death and He can do nothing to save them because, He wants to preserve their *free will?* He is bound by His own Word . . . ? This is not irony at work here, Michael, and I will dare to say it if no one else will—it is the pinnacle of arrogance. God is selfish and arrogant," he said defiantly. "Forgive me if I go too far," he paused, his brow bending upward with concern, softening his eyes while he asked almost pleadingly, "Why must High-Bourne battle against Legion, Michael? You cannot defeat me, for the same reason God cannot. The Great Lord allowed humans a choice and they chose—it is that simple, Michael. It was their choice, not yours, and not His . . . theirs." Lucifer did not want to provoke the General into a fight. He knew he'd possibly said too much already, so he lifted the air a bit, but continued to hone in on his real goal.

"You must think for yourself now, Michael. You have the power to. You have never felt the power of shadow embrace you . . . have you? The power of choice? The power to choose what you want and the courage to take it whether the Great Lord wants you to or not?" Lucifer chewed the words with slow deliberation. "I have," he said triumphantly. "And I can show you. Be your own general. Can you not see that we are alike, Michael? We are not mere mortals made from clay. We are Sons of fire—brothers, you and I. Look at yourself—one angel with the strength of many. You were never meant to serve. You were meant to rule! You know I speak the truth. You may be a general in heaven, but rule with me and I will make you a god." At this point, Lucifer impressed even himself. He subtly twisted half-truths while seamlessly adding logic. But the real poison of his words was cunning, so cunning an angel could fall for it. Michael's gifting of wisdom would ward him from any blatant temptation. To make him a lord of Baal-Shadow here and now was not the goal. The General would never willfully turn his heart against the Great Lord. Lucifer had accounted for that. Those were merely the top layers of the archdemon's deceit, a decoy to lure the General's attention while he carefully prepared the real trap. And so he did. He blabbed on openly with platitudes about Michael's potential, the power of shadow, and what Michael was *surely* missing out on. He used all of his guile to divert the archangel's attention while simultaneously doing his best to slither his way in the back door of Michael's consciousness. Carefully he chose each word, lavishing the General with the most unlikely of poisons. Praise . . . the poison was concealed inside affirmation and praise. Upon finishing, Lucifer waited . . . he watched, looking for a spark, for even the tiniest ember of pride, to catch fire in Michael's eyes. For he would surely know, and that was all it would take. One small sin of pride, and he would win without even drawing a sword, and heaven's general would fall before him like so many others.

But Lucifer had made a very big mistake, and his

arrogance would cost him dearly. To the General, the issue
had never been about his own power or his own strength
or even about defending the Prime Command. To the
General, it had nothing to do with embracing the shadow
or making his own way. In fact, it wasn't about him at all.
To the General, it was *all* about the child—the living Son of
the Great Lord of hosts. The General knew that Lucifer did
not understand this yet—but he was about to. Lucifer still
had no idea *why* he was present in Bethlehem this night.
In ignorance, he stared at the General, still waiting for his
poison to take effect.

Michael's eyes flickered and Lucifer's heart leaped
inside his chest. A sinister smile slowly twisted his mouth.
Cautiously he took a step forward.

*Have I done it? By the Silver Cord, have I felled heaven's
General? Ruined him with mere words?* His lips quivered with
anticipation.

CHAPTER 15: THIS ONE DEMON

The General surveyed his surroundings, fastidious as always, knowing the truth of the matter in his heart. He had carefully warded his mind with wisdom. He felt the words of the Dragon roll off of him like rain off a duck's back. Nothing good could come from that conversation, anyway. He knew that somewhere in the words of the blathering demon was the means to an end—a very bad end. So he used the time to think. Opening another pattern of concurrent thought was the easy part. What was hard, was mastering just how much prudence to give the mad demon. He dulled

Lucifer's voice down to an annoying buzz; just enough to understand. To ignore the elder demon entirely would just be folly. The past had proven Dragons to be quite capable, and nothing if not resourceful. However, the General had proven his own worth on the field of battle. He had few equals in the art of war and the list of those who had survived a campaign against him were even fewer. For his part, he was just Michael, plain and simple. To everyone else, he was Archistrategos, the master tactician. The Precepts of War were a part of him now, as surely as this broken world was a part of him. Lucifer rambled on as Michael's eyes swept across the battlefield in a blur, head swiveling efficiently. It felt so natural. Sadly, even the battlefield felt natural to him now. The Precepts of War were as natural as breathing or flying. *Patience of the Mountain—discern your enemy.* His head swiveled, measuring out the space above and around Lucifer, who was by his eye five hundred and ninety-four cubits from the Child.

Face of the Wind—gauge his might.

CHAPTER 15: THIS ONE DEMON

He scanned behind the archdemon, estimating distances and the response times of his ranks. Methodically, he weighed their strength, noting not only the distance of the Legion, but which ranks stood where, where the flyers were, the ones grounded, the ones with mounts and the ones without. He studied the front lines, their body language, how they stood on edge, tense, but not poised for attack. He knew they were waiting for a signal, and the signal had not come yet. He noted Lucifer leaning on his hind haunches, favoring his back right leg. But centuries of battle had trained him to know that Lucifer's body would shift before such a move would, or could, transpire. He counted with perfect accuracy the multitude of demons on the front lines every thirty seconds to see if any of their number had moved from their posts. Then he compared his numbers, especially his calculations of the Quintessence, with Mal'ak's numbers.

Mal'ak's Ta'ow eyes could see the numbers clearly without counting. His chestnut hide glistened under Bethlehem's pale moon as he nodded in relief. His numbers matched the General's perfectly. "Will the Quintessence manifest?" he asked, trying unsuccessfully to hide his concern from the link.

"Of course it will," the General barked. His voice was as hard as stone. Mal'ak didn't flinch, though—not too much. The gravel in the General's voice was not aimed at him, anyway. Sometimes, stone was the softest you could afford here in the Haze. Ripples fluttered the surface of the link, shadowing the General's thoughts, or what thoughts Mal'ak could track. Most were just orders, sent to the tribes, deliberated in varying tones of varying importance. But it wasn't about tone—not with the General. Authority itself girded the elder angel to the point of underpinning every word, even the most menial of his commands seemed spoken *and* regarded with the immovable certainty of a steel truss. He *was* every inch Archistrategos, The Great Tacticianer— the very *tip* of the sword. And to him everything was either illuminated or of the shadow. There was little in between. There were other thoughts, flittering by, however.

CHAPTER 15: THIS ONE DEMON

Calculating thoughts . . . *killing* thoughts. Mal'ak shuddered. The General knew more ways to kill a demon than Mal'ak thought possible. Some of them were not killing strikes as much as dismembering blows that left the demon still alive, but useless. And they all had names, "Strike of the Crane," "Edge of the spear." Wait! not names . . . Precepts. Light of the Dawn! *more* Precepts? Mal'ak's tufted ears drooped. He was still trying to figure out Bend like the Forest, not to mention the Quintessence, whatever that was.

'*The Quintessence is the miracle,*' the Chronicler's voice broke in, like the soft peal of bells. '*Without it, victory would remain . . . well, uncertain,*' he sniffed, obviously not caring for the thought too much.

'*But how do we know a miracle is going to happen today, if we don't know what that particular miracle is supposed to look like?*' asked Mal'ak.

'*You will know, because, today is primed for a miracle, and you will see because it is written within the numbers.*'

Mal'ak's brow pinched. '*Ugh, sometimes, you sound just

like another friend of mine,' he said, knuckling his forehead. The link carried a familiar rhythm now, an orange ripple that spread like the hint of laughter. Mal'ak had no idea where the Chronicler's position was on the battlefield in relation to his own and the General's, but he didn't have to see his face to know the Chronicler was amused. *Again,* thought Mal'ak.

'*Concerning the Precepts of War,*' the Chronicler continued, his voice receding, but still on the clear edge of laughter, '*we will defer to the General on that matter. I would leave you with a query to ponder though, a small pittance.*'

'*Okay . . .*' said Mal'ak, knowing the "small," question to ponder was probably well beyond his own reasoning.

'*Whose battle is this, Mal'ak? In whose war are we fighting? To answer that question, is to rest in all other questions, rather than wrestle with them.*' And with that, he was gone as quickly as he had come.

Wordsmiths. Mal'ak frowned, gripping his chin hair. *Their answers had more turns than a Crafter's puzzle.* At least the Precepts were *starting* to come to him now. Well, most of them. In truth, he knew them far better than he cared to admit. They were a part of him now. Dawn knows those "Precepts" had been beaten into his hide over the past few months of training—literally. He'd healed up nicely though. Of course, his wounds were nothing that a weave of spirit could not handle, but exhaustion was another matter. The Chronicler had warned him. "A weave of Spirit heals, but there is no magic for rest." Seven days he had stood in this spot. His head throbbed and there was pressure behind his eyes. He needed to shut them. He needed rest. Of course, that was impossible. They stood, watching what would be history's defining moment. The Epoch Horizon had brought them all to the very brink of war. Dawn's Light, who had time for sleep? So, wide eyed, he stood, rehearsing the Precepts of War, his head swiveling in tandem with the General's. However, for all the painful lessons he had acquired in training, there was still one Precept that eluded him. The third Precept, *Bend like the Forest*. Of course the

General would not tell him the interpretation of the third. O no . . . he had to figure it out on his own.

"The battlefield is your own mind Mal'ak," the General would say. "*There*, in the space *before* the sword is drawn, *that* is where victory keeps her secrets."

Mal'ak puffed breath through droopy eyebrows. The General was right, of course. There was so much at stake. Stirrings and Dragons, the Epoch Horizon—Dawn only knows how his own Calling was wrapped up in the middle of it all. If he was going to live to see it through, he dared not stop now. Not just for himself, but for the Child—especially for the Child. Mal'ak sighed, pulling at the hairs of his chin.

"*Patience of the Mountain*, discern your enemy," he whispered.

His head swiveled north. "*Face of the Wind*, gauge his might."

Only two procedures remained. *Bend Like the Forest* and *Conquer Like the Flame*. Mal'ak shuddered at the latter. That was easy. It meant the end was close. But for the life of him, he could not figure out *Bend Like the Forest*. It had to mean feign weakness, which was fairly easy for a Ta'ow, especially with Dragons running about. But the General had no weakness, period. Everyone knew that. So how do you pretend weakness when everyone knows you are strong? As far as *Consume Like the Flame*, Mal'ak's neck bristled at this Precept. If it came to war, the powers represented here could crack the planet in half. If it came to it, would there be anything left for flesh when the ashes cleared?

Well . . . three out of four Precepts would have to do for the moment, he thought. Maybe *Bend like the Forest* would come to him before the battle did and maybe, just maybe, *Consume Like the Flame* would not be needed at all this day. *The Dawn's favor, let it be so*, he thought.

It was nearing the seventh hour. Dawn was crowning the eastern hill-line of the small town already, dusting the clay brick houses in orange light. The Legion still had not moved, apart from the Dragon lord, and that was odd. Then, without warning, something rippled through the mind link that Mal'ak had sensed before, once in the Chronicler. An immense pool of sadness rippled along the tether, but this time, it was touched by surprise. The General recoiled, but it was too late. He might as well have laid his heart bare. Mal'ak not only sensed it, but the feeling was so intense, his own throat lumped up. *This should be private*, he thought with a twinge of sadness. The General was rigid steel . . . on the outside. On the inside, he was exposed by the link and affronted by the last thing either of them would have ever expected: his own emotions.

Tears formed on the rims of the General's eyes, threatening to spill over. The chiseled features of the stoic High-Bourne twisted in a struggle to keep his composure. His head fiercely battled his heart, and Archistrategos faltered. But only for a moment; it was over as quickly as it had begun. The General's dark brow narrowed downward as if to cut off his tears and give rise to something more useful. Something far more useful. Anger.

Anger welled up inside of him like a furnace, and the

flame in his eyes flared, burning away his tears just as quickly. Unbridled rage coursed through his veins as he cast his gaze upon Lucifer, and his heart ached with the memories of ten thousand battles washing over him. Ached for the war—for the dying and the damned, for the depthless evil and the vile corruption the Blight had unleashed upon children.

Dawn help me, thought Mal'ak. *He's damning children!*

Aye, grunted the General. *The Great Lord's children. All of this pain . . . because of this one demon.* The General's memories flashed, and Adam's humiliation flashed across the link, right on the heels of Eve's shame. The memory was sharp, to Mal'ak, it felt as if they were standing in the garden of Eden with them.

"Adam!" Mal'ak's voice quivered. He had never seen Adam like this before. Aging, and with a heart as broken as his body. And it was just like the General said. " It was all because of this one demon." The General's memories continued to mount, pulling them both in deeper. Mal'ak could almost feel Lucifer's delight. Corrupting the innocence of humans was akin to the purest of pleasures for him. And though it was only a memory, it sickened Mal'ak to watch. Lucifer gloated over them, over his best friends, like they were animals. Profaning that which bore the Great Lord's own image, that which was so precious.

The General stood, a tight-jawed pillar with wings, obviously wishing he could forget, but for some reason unknown to Mal'ak, he let his memory and the link forge ahead unmercifully. Mal'ak watched the first blood ever spilled, soaking into the earth hot and red, leaking life from the flesh of Adam's son, Able, as Samyaza clawed his way up from the pit of Baal-Shadow. Death was born that day, and pain was his harbinger. All because of this *one* demon. And the hackles on both of their necks stood erect as the centuries flash by and families were torn apart in the billions. Mal'ak lowered his eyes....

"Steady your gaze!" the General said brusquely. "Take courage, Mal'ak. I want you to *see* your enemy, and *never*, forget!"

CHAPTER 15: THIS ONE DEMON

It was then, that Mal'ak felt it. Something inside the General had died all those ages ago. For all his great strength, a well of sadness pooled in the General's heart. Mal'ak had never known sadness like this. It sat deep within the pools of the heart's anguish, a sadness that could never be plumbed with words. Sadness like this could only be felt. He'd felt the same thing when linked with the Chronicler. Strange, he'd never thought of it until now. That there could be a price to their power. And even stranger that restraint, of all things, might end up being the greatest of the General's own vast powers. The Prime Command was quickly becoming a much clearer concept to Mal'ak. Still, not interfering with human free will, was one thing, but having the General's power and having to stand by as women were violated by men with broken hearts was another. To feel the power of Light-Bringer blaze in your bare hands and yet having to stand aside and do nothing, *nothing*, while the world weeps.

He's right, Mal'ak thought, trying to steel his own heart. All of this sadness, all of this pain, was because . . . *of one . . . demon.*

The General's grip on Light-Bringer tightened.

271

Imrah Light-Bringer—if ever there was a weapon powerful enough to kill the Dragon lord, it was the legendary blade he held in his hands. That knowledge vexed him to the core. Words filled the breadth and width of the link that, to Mal'ak's eyes, resembled the lament of a prayer. No, pleading would be more accurate. The General had gone to the trouble of reliving the fall of humanity with one part of his mind, so Mal'ak could understand, and with another part of his mind, he was praying. Pleading with all of his might, begging the Great Lord to allow him to end it now—to let him strike *now!* The ember flame in his eyes smoldered, burning away the last vestiges of tears, leaving no doubt to the answer the Great Lord had given him. Revenge was the Great Lord's province alone, every High-Bourne knew that. But Mal'ak had to wonder at the rage coursing through the General. Archistrategos stared at Lucifer with a mighty hate that would as soon kill the elder demon as have breath and life. If the fetters were ever loosed from the General, if God's hand of restraint were to ever release Michael the archangel's wrath, Mal'ak supposed that nine hells would not stop him from cutting that demon's head off, or die trying. But as always, the General never questioned his King, even when he did not understand the why of the matter.

****

Lucifer's eyes still rested upon the General, as defiant as ever, though his patience was running thin. "Answer me," Lucifer whispered, as he slowly chanced another step closer. "Who do you serve now?" The General moved one hand to the inside of his feather-cloth tunic and loosened the folds, just enough to reveal a dark slender object dangling loosely from his neck on a golden Ta'ow crafted chain. The shaft of a horn lay pitch black against the High-Bourne's bronze skin. Its crystalline edges glistened, jagged and broken on one end, and came to a sharp point at the other. In the horn's broken center blood had coagulated mixed with green swirls. The General glanced down at the ebon horn he had ripped free from Lucifer's head so long ago in the Age of the Turning. His head was awash with memories as he fingered the length of its shaft, then abruptly, he stopped. Michael tapped the broken edge of the horn with his forefinger. A smile nearly split his face as he lifted his gaze from the horn in his hand to stare straight at Lucifer. It was not a kind smile, but the sort of smile one gives when relishing a moment. To Lucifer's horror, the General's smile quickly faded to a gritted tooth snarl. The General let loose a guttural war cry, deep and unearthly. It put an end to the conversation and brought to bear his intentions, leaving no doubt, *exactly* where the General's fealty lay.

The High-Bourne of his clan, some four billion angels, snapped ready and roared a sonorous rejoinder to their general's call. Wild-eyed, the General peered down the front lines of the Legion, letting his gaze fall on any demon who would dare meet it. Again, he cut loose with a visceral war cry, having the look of a celestial general gone mad.

CHAPTER 16:
WAR

Fear trickled down the lines of the Legion. Restless, they squirmed under the sound of the General's voice. Lucifer had his answer, and more. The General was done with talk. Michael knew that the real answer would not come from *his* mouth. It was not his place, but he was going to enjoy every moment of delivering the message.

An explosion of white light erupted from the General's body as Halo manifested, forming just above the General's head. In its brightness, Michael unfurled his huge wings, which spanned more than fourteen cubits in length.

He crouched low. The muscles in his legs knotted, then flexed, catapulting him forty spans into the air.

"Aid me!" Lucifer screamed, and four Mawgore charged from behind him, their bulbous yellow eyes veined red and riddled with hate, converged on the General. The General reached with his mind to Mal'ak.

'*Stay with the King. We must wait upon the Quintessence.*'

Mal'ak's ears lay flat against the back of his skull. His chest expanded and his hands curled into fists that could hew stone from a mountain. He spoke, and hardly recognized the steel in his own voice. '*Neither the Mawgore, nor the Dragon lord himself shall lay a finger on my Lord and King. The Dawn be with you, General.*'

The General released the link and turned his full attention to the four Mawgore coming straight for him. Quickly, he took measure of the space between them and him and whispered, "*Consume Like the Flame.*" Light emanated from Halo just above his head. Shafts of pure white light spread before him like threads on a weaver's loom, each ray traveling to a different location. All he needed were the right locations. There was no room for error. His huge wings held him aloft, beating the air: *thoom, thoom, thoom.* He reached for the light, then he was gone. The General moved at transluminant speed. A move as bold as it was dangerous.

Mal'ak's brow bent inward, apprehension wrinkling his forehead. The High-Bourne tribes were accustomed to using the paths of light, but Halo was only used for travel, and usually over great distances. To use Halo in combat— it had never been attempted before. If the General were to misjudge the distance, if he held on too long, he could end up light years past his mark, the Mawgore, and even past the solar system itself.

Lucifer gasped as the General moved with a speed and force almost unimaginable, even by angel standards. He blinked in and out of view, oscillating between what Lucifer's eyes could see and what he knew should be impossible. His frame moved near light speed while his sword ripped through the air, setting it ablaze as he flew. The flame in his wake was the only evidence of where he was or had been moments before. The General flew confidently in his God-given impossible task, pulled by the paths of light and feeling the luminous energy race under the touch of his fingertips. As he flew, he cut an intricate pattern of runes made of flame into the air, a warding hedge of protection. The warding circle of flame would be absolute in height and depth and could not be crossed from a high vantage or from underneath. In this, he was confident. His unease, however, bordered on the fringes of worry when he thought of who would be left inside the blazing circle of fire when he finished. But as always, he went on, never questioning his orders. He continued cutting the swath of fire in the air. It began to the right, then traveling seven cubits behind the child, the General arced in a great circle far behind where Lucifer and the Mawgore stood. He blazed a cobalt trail right past the front lines, effectively cutting Lucifer off from the rest of the Legion. However, to his growing concern, the great circle of fire, when completed, would effectively cut off the High-Bourne tribes from the child as well. All that would remain in the circle of flame from his ranks would be Mal'ak, the Chronicler and himself. "It *will* be enough," the General said resolutely. "*We* will be enough!" He reiterated the words, as if he needed reassuring himself.

The Mawgore no longer pursued him. This was of no great surprise to Michael, though. He was moving far too swiftly for the filthy beasts to keep pace. Then a whisper, soft, like a feather falling on the breeze, touched his ears. The warding of wisdom pulled hard at him. Discernment opened his mind and its revelation gripped his heart like a vice as he realized who the beasts had set their sights upon.

"No!" Michael roared. His voice was strained. In his long life, Michael feared nothing in all of existence, save one: that he would fail his King. He wrestled with that secret fear now, realizing full well that Lucifer was channeling a spell, exploiting his deepest fears this very moment. The fear's strength was reinforced by the presence of the Mawgore. The Fear Beasts drew upon the spell's effects in reciprocal lust, so hungry to devour the fears of an archangel, so hungry to taste the terror of a God Child. The General's warding of wisdom held, as wisdom always does, but he felt fear press in on his mind, its fingers scraping loud against the outside of his wards, trying to find a way inside of him.

They attacked the General and his King in tandem, but the General's mind remained intact. He watched the first two hell beasts charge Mal'ak while the second pair veered, barreling straight for the child. Michael did not think, he acted. Tucking his wings close, he corkscrewed in the air, loosing his grip on Halo's light. He searched between milliseconds for a path of light that would intersect with the two Mawgore. They ran abreast of one another, charging full bore toward the child.

The General's move was born of pure instinct. His body was still careening through Halo at near transluminant speed when he abandoned the first path and reached out for another leading directly to the Mawgore. He reached, and it felt as if Halo might tear his arm free from his shoulder. His jaw locked in determination. He gritted his teeth through the pain and spread his wings, stretching them outward as far as he could. He extended them, hardening them to a flattened razor's edge. His advance was as silent and deadly as a hawk plummeting toward prey. Light-Bringer hummed in his ears. He skimmed the ground, barely knee high, and held fast to Halo's light. It slung him with such velocity that the Mawgore, for a brief moment, ran on nubs, not realizing that the General's wings had cleaved their legs clean from their hairless bodies. High pitch screams rang from their throats, and their useless bodies contorted, trying to stand without legs while the putrid stink of their essence soaked the ground. The General released his grip on the light, angled his wings in sharply, and pulled up, alighting upon an outcropping of boulders to survey the battlefield in search of the Quintessence. Lucifer stood five hundred and ninety-three cubits from the Holy Child.

The archdemon had improvised tactically. Lucifer's Fear Beasts, though dealt with, ensured the General would be unable to finish his line of defense. The circle of fire was incomplete. A full one-fourth of its western section lay open and unprotected.

The drums of war beat out a primal cadence with the Legion's lust for battle, and the horns of Zion pierced the night sky in defiant riposte as both High-Bourne and Legion raced toward the gaping path in the flame. The High-Bourne arrived first. Some cloaked, some moving out in the open, but all stone-faced fury. Each one moved through the Precepts of War in rapid precision. Lancers raised the first line of defense. Light-based cannons lit up the night sky, firing into the throng of Legion, punching holes twenty-one cubits wide in the ground. Forces split, war was being fought on two fronts: on the ground and in the air. The High-Bourne on the ground had dug in quickly, trying to plug the gap in the warding wall of flame the General had carved, but the sheer number of Legion pushing in on them was mind numbing. There was no Precept for War on this scale.

Trogs darkened the northern skyline, and Kolossos with their huge horns charged the front lines like giant battering rams, with more pushing in every second. It was as if two angry seas had risen to battle, and their waves were lost to each other in the clash. Whole companies of High-Bourne Sentries were swept away, awash in a sea of angels and demons. As bodies piled on top of one another, more and more High-Bourne pushed into the fray, desperately trying to shore up the hole in the flame, shore it up with their own bodies if need be.

A group of seven Sentries uncloaked. One of them, a broad-shouldered High-Bourne with bronzed hair, thrust the Lion Banner into the ground, baring his teeth. Without warning a golden blur, swooped out of the sky and the banner keeper was gone. Tannin scooped him up in his toothy maw and shook him like a rag doll. The Lion banner fell in slow motion toward the ground, but before it ever touched soil another High-Bourne, another of the seven, scooped it up, holding it high. *He* was the banner keeper now. Jaw set, he waved it proudly.

"For the King!" he shouted skyward at Tannin. A

Bronze Dragon swooped in, catching the new keeper in its maw. The five remaining Sentries immediately cloaked around the beast, disappearing, slashing, reappearing, dodging and doing it all over again, pacing through the Precepts in a dance with death. The Bronze was thick and well-muscled, having two horns and triangle shaped scales rather than the diamond shaped scales of his kin. Bronze Dragons were smallest among Dragon kin, but still a Dragon, nonetheless, and plenty large enough to make a meal of any High-Bourne Sentry. But this did not stop the Shade of His Hand. All five High-Bourne dove in at once, slashing at the Dragon's vulnerable underbelly.

The Dragon's maw was still full with their brother. Angel essence leaked from the corners of its oversized mouth. The Bronze tried to bear the keeper skyward, but the Keeper was far from dead—and clever. He hardened his wings to razored points, angling them outward against the impact of the bite, so the Dragon could not close its mouth all the way without piercing its own jaws, but also could not open its mouth wide enough to release around the High-Bourne's razored wings. For the moment, it was a deadly stalemate. Every time the Bronze would spread his wings to fly, the Sentries would uncloak, slashing at the un-plated ribbing under its wings, keeping him earth bound—for the moment. The keeper struggled for freedom inside the mouth of the beast. His right side was pinned, crushed between two huge fangs in the back of the Bronze's mouth. He had already lost his sword down its throat in the initial assault, but he was busy hacking gashes into of the roof of the beast's mouth with his bladed gauntlet. The blade was not long enough for a killing blow, but it hurt, that much was certain by the roars and shudders of each stabbing blow. Suddenly, the Bronze lurched, spewing hot bile from its throat, covering the High-Bourne keeper in acid. The keeper twisted in agony, but kept stabbing as his skin, skin as hard as stone, melted away. If he screamed, only the other five High-Bourne heard it through the link.

The Dragon roared after swallowing the remains of the keeper.

"Dead!" he screamed, pointing a taloned finger at the

five Sentries. "I will feassst on you all," he said, his voice like cold death.

The Sentries were not archangels, but they were still Shade of His Hand, and not one of them knew what it meant to back down. They cloaked again, about to charge, when something large rolled onto the battlefield, a wheel within a wheel—a Seraph's wheel. The wheel floated in a slow spin while the multi-eyed Seraph's other half drifted to its side. Seraphim are a two-bodied single consciousness, a higher caste of angel.

This drew concern wide across Bronze's face. Neither the Legion nor High-Bourne had ever seen a Seraph away from the throne of the Great Lord, much less on a battlefield.

The Bronze bowed up, swelling its chest, defiance gleaming in his beady black eyes.

"Come to die, too, Seraph?" he jeered with a smile, teeth still wet with the keeper's essence. The Seraph tilted its head to one side as its six diaphanous wings full of eyes drummed the air effortlessly. Its wheel began to spin faster at its side. Softly at first, then louder and faster, louder and faster and faster it spun. Lightning arced, latticing the inner portions that spun in a counter direction to the outer spinning wheel. The Bronze took an uncertain step back, the ground shuddered, and—BOOM!

Gliding over, the Seraph landed amidst the five High-Bourne. Stooping down, the elder angel picked up the Lion Banner in one hand and with another hand, he pointed a finger toward the charred patch of earth that used to be the Bronze, and said, "Dead . . . ."

"For the King!" the Seraph roared.

The High-Bourne tribes erupted. "For the King! For the King!" they cheered as they pushed harder into the throng.

****

The General turned his eyes from the mouth of the flame toward the child in time to see Mal'ak, head lowered, in full charge. Even from this distance, the General felt the powerful stride of Mal'ak's hooves pounding the soil. He was on course for the remaining two Mawgore. Michael watched the first demon rear up just before impact and Mal'ak seized the moment by angling his huge horns, catching the Beast between its ribs. He drove them in deep. The Mawgore screeched in pain with the muted grind of bone against horn as Mal'ak's horns sunk deep inside its belly.

The other horn he drove straight into the mouth of the hell beast. It stove up inside the roof of its oversized maw. The Mawgore bit down hard. Its yellow teeth made a horrible scraping sound, like that of stone drawn against marble, furrowing deep grooves into Mal'ak's horn. Desperately, the Mawgore tried to stop him from driving them deeper.

Mal'ak did not hesitate, though. He pressed the advantage as the General had taught him. Using his considerable strength, in one swift motion, he worked his arms around the Mawgore's lower back, toward the thick of its tail, and heaved. The beast's yellow eyes widened as its four legs left the ground. Mal'ak's arms and neck bulged as he hefted the gluttonous demon into the air. While he lifted with his horns, he pulled inward with his arms until the almond horn ensconced in the roof of the beast's mouth shot out the back of its head. The other horn slid completely through its belly, bursting out of its back. The Mawgore wriggled, screaming in agony. It clawed at Mal'ak's horns buried in its gut and mouth, trying desperately to free itself.

Mal'ak's stomach turned as viscous fluid dripped on his face. Swiftly, he hoisted the beast high above his head. With his horns still sheathed in its gut and mouth, he braced his hooves in the soil and shook his broad head back and forth so violently, Michael heard the demon's body snap and pop, and then with a great crack the Fear Beast sagged lifeless atop Mal'ak's horns.

Mal'ak slung the demon to the soil like a limp rag and stomped the earth with one cloven hoof, *boom, boom*. Then he placed it squarely upon the demon's neck. There came another loud crack. Raising his horns high, he wheeled around, preparing to engage the other beast in battle when his leg gave way. With a grunt, he collapsed to the ground. Mal'ak felt as if his leg were set to open flame. Instinctively, he reached for the pain, only to put his hand inside a wound that extended halfway down his leg. It was deep—very deep. In its death throes the Mawgore had narrowly missed disemboweling him. Essence bled freely from the deep gash, but strangely, it mattered little to Mal'ak. His heart ran wild with the heat of battle and Dawn help him, he would fight from his knees if he had to. However, it became quickly apparent that he might not have to. He knew the other Fear Beast should have been upon him by now, but the remaining Mawgore had stopped in its tracks, well short of where Mal'ak stood. Though the General was too far off to hear, Mal'ak's tufted ears pricked upward when he heard a soft melody floating on the wind. The sound was faint, a haunting whisper that rose and fell on the breeze. It was complex, yet relaxing, like the sound of water. A song of dreams mixed with the voice of an angel.

CHAPTER 16: WAR

The Mawgore seemed frozen, its feet rooted in place by the song's strange lethargy. Alone, it stood completely still, panting in labored breaths with the blank air of uncertainty. Something stirred in those glazed-over yellow eyes . . . *fear*. That was its final expression.

The air beside the Mawgore quivered. Light bent inward to reveal a slender hand with a blade just under its throat. Gabriel slit the Hell Beast from gullet to gizzard. Essence spewed forth in a repulsing stench as its body slumped to the ground and its broad head nearly rolled away. Everything was happening terribly fast. It was becoming increasingly difficult for either side to keep up. Suddenly, Gabriel's voice broke through to the General's mind, but not in his usual calm. It held a subtle edge that belied the tremendous strain they were all under.

"The King!"

CHAPTER 17:
THE QUINTESSENCE

Gabriel all but shouted across their mind link. *'Lucifer has shielded his mind with Shadow-Bind. I cannot stop him from here!'*

'Go,' the General said. *'I will see to the Dragon lord myself. You have to mend the flame, Gabriel. The hedge must be complete. The Legion cannot pass if I am to deliver the message as our Lord sees fit.'*

The Chronicler did not have to take orders from the General, at least to Mal'ak's understanding. His station was unique among the High-Bourne tribes. Regardless, neither would allow pride to interfere with asking for help. Gabriel knew the General had a direct word from the King, and so deference was in order. Through the link, Mal'ak noted a subtle quiver in the General's voice. A quiver that he felt and that Gabriel recognized not just from the link, but from eons of war and friendship with the archangel. A quiver born not of fear, but of unbridled fury, whose sole purpose for breath and life was absolute fealty to his King. Fury was about to be released.

Lucifer took one . . . more . . . step.

"The Quintessence has aligned in our favor," the General growled. "We wait no longer." He bristled with God's glory resting upon him.

Mal'ak marveled at the terrible power coursing through Light-Bringer and watched it spill over onto the General, who embraced it with unmitigated poise. His hands trembled with the touch of the God-Flow upon him. No words were spoken between them as the General turned to face the Dragon.

CHAPTER 17: THE QUINTESSENCE

Lucifer stood perfectly in line with the law of the Quintessence, precisely five hundred and ninety-two cubits in front of the General. It was time.

When their eyes locked, the General's changed from ember flame to a cold blue burn, matching the cobalt flame of Light-Bringer's blaze. Lucifer took one step backward as the General took five huge strides forward and shot headlong into the air, exhilarated as he accelerated under the embrace of God's touch. Quickly leaving the ground behind, he arced far above the Child and Mal'ak. Then, raising Light-Bringer high above his head, he pulled his wings in close to his body, banked sharply toward the earth, and dove like living starlight toward the Dragon.

Stunned, Lucifer stood in open mouthed silence. Michael was coming for him, and he carried with him the God-Flow. There was one chance—*only* one chance against the General. Light-Bringer had to go. Somehow, the weapon had to be removed. Quickly, he turned from the General to face the Child and of all things, a *Ta'ow*. Sheol's flames, why would a Crafter be fighting with High-Bourne? With a growl Lucifer shoved the thought away. There was no time. From the corner of his eye, he could see the General plummeting toward him. Mere seconds were all that remained before impact. Lucifer inhaled a deep rasp of a breath and blew with all of his might. Hellfire spewed from his mouth, racing hot across the ground, consuming everything in its path. The air ignited under the immense heat, but strangely, the Ta'ow did not move.

Mal'ak held his post beside the holy Child, as the General had instructed. The truth was, he could no longer feel his lower leg anymore, and his hip felt like it was already on fire, so he knelt. He could still do *that*—if he put his weight on his good side. The ground trembled. It looked like the horizon had caught on fire and that it would sweep the world clean before long. He looked down at the Child.

"What is my calling, Little One?" he asked with more calm than he actually felt. The Child seemed at ease. Its tiny chest rose and fell in sleep, as if the world itself were not about to burn. Mal'ak looked to the hammer. "Please," he pleaded, pulling at its shaft. "What is it that I most need?" The old weapon wouldn't budge. Since the battle had begun, it had lain dormant—rooted in the ground beside the Child. It had not budged since.

"If you're so attuned to what I need *most*, then why in heaven's name won't you tell me?" The air shimmered around them. The blaze of the horizon filled his peripheral. As if in answer, Shamayin rooted itself even deeper into the earth, its boughs sprouting along the ground, curving up and around the contour of the feed trough, all but cradling the Holy Child. Mal'ak's mouth thinned. "You're staying. I get it. So, if we stay, then what I need most is . . . ."

The General's words from their time spent in the Narrows echoed within his memory. "Let *courage* rise, Blacksmith. Let *courage* rise!"

Mal'ak's eyes widened. "Dawn's Light!" The answer suddenly seemed obvious. "*Courage!*" he whispered. "Sometimes what we need *most* . . . is *courage!*"

With the horizon almost upon him he crawled on all fours, dragging his leg. Drawing strength from the General's words, Mal'ak drew himself up, gently placing his huge frame over the Child's tiny body. Gritting his teeth through the pain, he whispered in the babe's ear, "I am Towr Mal'akim of the Ta'ow, High-Bourne of the Most High . . . and no demon . . . shall . . . *touch* you, my Lord!" It was first time he'd ever thought of himself as High-Bourne, much less spoke it aloud. It was a good thought. Tears, his first tears born from joy, streamed down his muzzle. Hellfire howled in his ears, rumbling the earth like thunder. Mal'ak folded his arms tight around the Child and braced himself.

Without warning, a streak of blue and white smashed into the ground in front of him, leaving a black smoldering crater. In its center stood the General, holding Light-Bringer high in both hands. Like a waterfall converging upon a stone, hellfire parted on either side of Light-Bringer. Mal'ak raised his head and gave glory to God. He touched Michael's mind for just a moment with his own and said,

CHAPTER 17: THE QUINTESSENCE

'Get him, General. For the King!'

With that, a river of flame, the like of which Mal'ak had never seen before, blotted out the sky. The General did not answer, but Mal'ak could feel him along the link. He was a ball of iron will, with a lion's heart. The flames parted on either side of them and struck the warded hedge behind them. With a roar, it pushed fiercely against the General, melting the ground around them to cinder and ash.

Then the General pushed back. His first step was slow, but steady. He took another, then another, his bronzed feet hammering the soil like bludgeoning pistons with each stride. The next few came more quickly. In no time he was at a steady gait, running against the torrential blaze, each stride furrowing the ground beneath him. For long moments, the flames continued to flow from the Dragon lord's mouth, but the General would not be denied. He forged on, relentless, his face set like a bronze golem, as he pushed headlong through hellfire. One feeling, one overriding thought transcended all others: His King was in danger, and the General was invincible.

The gap between them was closing, and Lucifer was in a panic. There were no more clever plans, or cunning offers. And eventually, he must inhale to continue the flame.

The General was close now. So close, Lucifer could see those unyielding blue eyes, even through hell fire. They bore into him. He inhaled as quickly as he could, but the flame wavered, and the General struck. Thrusting his wings forward, Michael launched a barrage of light infused quills so fast, Lucifer was unable to volley another breath.

He felt one sink deep into his throat. It was lodged so far in, only the tip of the shaft shown. A glimmering sliver contrasted against the Dragon's ruby hide. Lucifer roared in pain, clawing at his throat. He spun around, exposing the thicker scales of his back, just in time to feel another volley of the General's quills smash against him. Even though most of them did not penetrate the thicker scales lining his back, each quill struck the elder demon with searing pain. The light infused in them left his armored hide welted, raised with purple around the edges. Instinctively, Lucifer leaped high into the air. Clawed hands still clutching his throat, he unfurled his massive wings and flew toward the Legion and the open path of the warded flame.

The General already had the momentum, though. He had not slowed a step, even when loosing the quills from his wings. He moved with perfect precision and deadly grace as he leaped into the air. With one downward stroke of his wings, he propelled himself forward and tackled the great Dragon. The bronze skin of the High-Bourne met the thick, scaled hide of the Dragon lord in a tremendous clash, iron smashing against stone. Sparks erupted in brilliant swirls and tiny yellow motes showered the ground.

Lucifer reached for the sky, still desperately trying to fly, but the General's momentum sent them both careening out of control. The ground quaked as they collided with the earth and the force of the impact broke the two apart, but the General recovered from the fall almost instantly and was already on his feet. Out of reflex, Lucifer opened his mouth, straining to exhale, but only thin wisps of smoke came out. The shaft in his throat burned like he had swallowed holy water, and the flame would not pass it. The quill was lodged so that he could scarcely breathe, and hellfire was nigh impossible. The General had landed on the far side of him and was charging again. Lucifer found himself caught between the General and the Holy Child. Realization dawned on him. The General was pushing him backward.

Sheol's flames! He's pushing me toward the child, he thought, astounded.

"What do you want from me?" Lucifer screamed, his voice garbled because of the bladed quill lodged in his gullet. Lucifer ground his teeth, enraged by the General's continued silence. "I'll feed on that baby's essence before its life of flesh comes to an end," he sneered, and curled back his lips, brandishing long rows of black teeth the length of a man's leg. He lunged. His long neck cut through the air with blinding speed toward the General's throat, only to bite down upon air.

Chapter 17: The Quintessence

The General's movements were as fluid as water snaking down a riverbed. He sidestepped the Dragon's bite by mere inches. Calling on all of his God-given strength, he swung Imrah Light-Bringer. The blade arced through the air, screaming its way toward Lucifer with unerring accuracy. However, just before its edge reached his skull, the General flipped the blade over so that the flat of Light-Bringer struck him flat across the back of his scaly head. With a mighty clap, the blow sent him airborne, and his entire body ignited in the blue flame of the God-Flow. A tormented howl escaped the throat of the great demon. His limp body flew through the air and landed in a heap, by the General's eye, exactly five hundred and ninety-two cubits from where he stood. Unexpectedly, Michael heard the sound of Gabriel's voice bombarding his mind.

'General! We can hold them no longer. The Legion have breached the wall. I did not make it in time—'

The General interrupted him in smooth even tones.

Anno Domini

'Gabriel, you must stop them. The Quintessence stands in our favor. The Dragon lord is in position this very moment. Do what you must, but find a way to stop them, now!'

CHAPTER 18:
REVELATION

Direct contact with Light-Bringer had burned Lucifer's hide unlike anything he had felt before. He was immune to most weapons. Even those weapons carried by the High-Bourne tribes, he usually possessed some resistance to. But this... *this* weapon, burned far deeper than his scales. He could feel the God-Flow inside him, scalding his innards. Lucifer lay on the ground, dazed and unable to gain his footing. He knew the General was coming, but his head throbbed so bad he couldn't think. Sheol's flames, especially the back of his skull where Light-Bringer had struck him. Willing himself up on all fours, Lucifer raised his head, only to have the General crash down on him again with bone crushing force.

He landed squarely upon Lucifer's long neck, straddling him at the base of his skull. Upon landing, the General had tapered his wings, hardening them into V-shaped points. He drove them deep into the earth underneath him, on either side of Lucifer's neck, pinning the Dragon lord's head securely to the ground. Lucifer dared not move. He felt the General's huge legs clamp down on his neck and the razor edge of the High-Bourne's wings sharp against his throat. Keeping his neck and head as still as he could, Lucifer clawed at the General desperately. Viciously, he bludgeoned Michael's back with his tail, but the General's wings had hardened into an impenetrable canopy. Lucifer cursed. His blows might as well have been rain against the General's wings. Without any warning, the General's body tensed. Instinctively, Lucifer sunk his talons in the earth and braced for an impact that never came—

at least not how he had imagined it. What happened was worse, far worse than any beating from the General's hands could ever be.

Lucifer stood at the fringes of revelation: why he was here; why they were *all* here. The General was about to show him. However, not with fighting. The answer would come, the decree would be made, from the Word of God.

The General held Imrah Light-Bringer high in both hands, poised above the Dragon's head. He paused as if inspecting something. Then, with tremendous force, he drove Light-Bringer downward, sheathing it into the ground, halfway to the hilt, and no more than half an inch from Lucifer's snout. The ground heaved upward, then collapsed on itself with a thump. Fissures perforated the scorched soil, boiling in tiny circles where the blade had penetrated the earth.

Dazed by the General's assault, Lucifer could not seem to puzzle out why his head still rested upon his shoulders. Above all, he dared not gaze upon the power of

Imrah Light-Bringer. He could feel that eyeless stare looking right through him.

Thoom-Thoom . . . Thoom-Thoom . . . Thoom-Thoom.

It vibrated the end of his snout, thumping the ground with a droning pulse. It pounded the earth just in front of his face, like the rise and fall of God's own heartbeat.

Thoom-Thoom . . . Thoom-Thoom . . . Thoom-Thoom.

He clenched his eyes as tight as he could, then an iron grip took hold of his horns. Terror stabbed his stomach. The terror of losing a part of himself to the General again overcame all other rationale. He howled, thrashing, panic renewing his limbs with new strength. But the General's arms, imbued with the strength of his *own* calling, didn't budge. The General actually managed a wide grin, when he heard the voice of an angel break out in song. It was unmistakable. Gabriel was singing. And it was not a whisper—not this time. It was magnificent. The Chronicler's voice soared with the long forgotten melodies of the Old Tongue, written by the Great Lord himself. The master musician held nothing back. Reciting the ancient canticles, he guided the flows with a skill not seen since the Age of the Turning.

"For unto us a child is born, unto us a son is given: and the government shall be upon his shoulders: and his name shall be called Wonderful, Counselor, The mighty God, The everlasting Father, The Prince of Peace. Of the increase of his government and peace there shall be no end, upon the throne of David, and upon his kingdom, to order it, and to establish it with judgment and with justice from henceforth-even forever."

The raucous melody spread across the battlefield. Praise of the Child seemed to mount like an avalanche. But as it did, something came with it, something that had been missing for four centuries. "Of all the places," the General said, shaking his head. "Joy . . . here?" A fat gluttonous demon with a pinched face almost lost his chin, his mouth fell open so wide. "The *Quintessence,*" whispered Mal'ak. "The Dawn Bringer be praised, it has to be!"

'*Can you feel that?*' asked Mal'ak, through the link. '*Is*

that . . . joy?' He looked down at the Child still nestled in his arms. "You would spread us a table, here? In the very presence of our enemies?" Mal'ak muttered. As if in answer, more High-Bourne joined in the Chronicler's song. Joy radiated from the Child like heat from the sun. *'It's coming from Him.' Mal'ak gasped. 'He's warm!'*

'Aye,' the General chimed in, astonishment clear in his own voice. 'He's affecting everything.'

The ancient language broken by Lucifer at the Age of the Turning had somehow manifested through the link. Every High-Bourne on the battlefield could hear it. The General let out a belly laugh. Of course, it was completely impossible, but that was the Quintessence. A bona fide miracle when all seemed lost. And that was probably just the beginning, if history served as any reminder. Seven, and only seven minds could bind to a link. That was the rule. Anymore and you would lose clarity. And clarity on the battlefield could mean the difference between living or dying. Or perhaps the greater miracle was that none of them, aside from the Word Smith, could even begin to understand a single utterance of the Great Song of Songs. But there it was, a song heard by four billion angels. Their voices shook the ground with the Creator's song.

Mal'ak's skin pebbled under his chestnut coat. He pushed himself up from the Child, raising his own voice to the fray, when all of a sudden, he heard the Chronicler whisper, '*Now is the time, and the time is now.*'

Mal'ak's head jerked straight up. '*What did you just say?*'

'*I said . . .* Now is the time, and the time is now.*'*

'*What does that mean?*' asked Mal'ak, swallowing hard.

'*I do not know,*' said the Chronicler, compassion softening his voice. '"*What I do know, is that our General's hands are full, and that I cannot draw on an ounce more of the God-Flow and hope to survive.*'

'*I'm just Ta'ow. I don't know what else to do,*' said Mal'ak.

'*Yes, you are Ta'ow. The only Ta'ow to hear a Stirring. The only Ta'ow with the Son of God in his arms, and the only High-Bourne I see on the battlefield at the moment whose Calling is Sacrosanct.*'

Mal'ak's bushy eye brows wilted to his cheeks, as he felt the Chronicler's presence fade from the link.

Seeing the Child asleep in his arms, Mal'ak couldn't help but smile.

"My legs betray me, little One, but I suppose you already knew that." He leaned in closer. "Every step has been ordained, hasn't it? From the Stirring, to Leviathan's jaws, all the way here to you." He pursed his mouth. "But . . . if You have purposed my steps, then why do I not see it, my Lord? If You would but widen my gaze, I would see Your glory this day. I would see it poured out, but I have nothing left to offer You but my life." A chill went out of him along with those words. He rolled them around slowly in his head, weighing the sums of what he had just spoken. The truth was, he did not have to steel his mind. Not for this—not for his King. As always, his heart had made the decision, his mind just had to catch up. Mal'ak leaned in closer and whispered, "Take it! If that is what you require, take it, while there is courage left in me. Come get Your glory!" he said, pressing his lips against the Child's ear. "Come get Your glory, my Lord! My life for yours...Honor and Strength, for *you* my King."

Mal'ak felt a tug about his neck.

"Dawn's Light, you're awake," Mal'ak said, incredulously. "You can see me!"

Humans were all but blind to the Spirit realm, and that had always been the way of it. Probably to preserve the Prime Command. But not this Child. This Child was born of both flesh and spirit, knit together in divinity, and had claims in both worlds like nothing else in existence. Brown eyes swung between Mal'ak and the amulet hanging about his neck. "The Tetragrammaton?" Mal'ak's brow climbed upward as the Child's tiny hand rose unsteadily into the air toward the round disk. At the touch of His finger, the amulet jumped to life. Light drew across its clear blue surface, and it shimmered like water.

All at once, Mal'ak could see. Not just the Stirring that had brought him here, but by the Dawn, he could see *everything*. He could see the road that had brought him here by the Stirring and the intertwining choices that connected to that road. He could see the choices he had made, and all of the possibilities of the choices he *could* have made. But to his surprise, all of his choices and all of the roads somehow led to one place . . . here, to the Epoch Horizon. He could see the amulet for what it *really* was, and he laughed out loud when it started to rain. "The amulet," he said, astonished. "*You* wanted the amulet for the rain!"

"By the Silver Cord, it bears *Your* name, little One; a single piece of Your name." Mal'ak marveled at the revelation. What safer place to hide an utterance of God's own name? Who would ever think to look inside the jaws of Leviathan. *Who would dare?* he thought. Then he blushed, remembering it was his own neck that the great Oracle hung about. Mal'ak looked down at the amulet resting in the Child's hands. It was only an utterance, but if names in the Old Tongue confer power, then what kind of power could one utterance of the Dawn Bringer's name hold? There is no other name given among man *or* angel above *this* name. Mal'ak suddenly looked at the babe like he was seeing him for the first time.

"We're not here to save *you*, are we little one? You're here to save them," he said, looking at Mary, who was caressing her baby, still oblivious to the world at war around her.

"We're just the witnesses," said Mal'ak, his ears fidgeting in a flutter. "But . . . how? How can you be so weak yet, so strong?"

Mal'ak's ears stopped fidgeting and pointed straight up. "*Bend like the Forest*," he said, gripping a handful of chin hair. "By the Silver Cord! *I'm Bend like the Forest*." He smacked Shamayin on the roots. Mal'ak wasn't sure if it was wisdom's subtle whisper, the Tetragrammaton, or the fact that he alone stood on a battlefield with the most important child in history, but he knew his purpose now, just like he did in the Narrows. It was as plain as the hammer was to the anvil. *Bend like the Forest* was

319

interpreted as feign weakness; any High-Bourne who knew the Precepts knew that. He just hadn't known how to apply it—until now.

"*I am* . . . the weakness?" he said breathlessly. A Ta'ow on the battlefield with a baby . . . Could there be a target any more luring for a Dragon than that? "I am *Bend like the Forest*," he said, laughing in spite of himself. He did not know whether to marvel at the General's tactical prowess or be offended that *he* was the one offered up as *Bend like the Forest*. Then he looked down at the Child. "No—we are both *Bend like the Forest*." Their eyes met, unblinking, and Mal'ak froze, transfixed while the Child's gaze held him. A gaze so innocent, yet holding all secrets beyond the far sides of eternity.

Bethlehem fell out from under Mal'ak, the war, everything, suddenly, just washed away. He was a speck, a grain of sand before an ocean of fire. A cross stood before him now, ablaze in glory. He could not determine its height, nor width, even by the lines of his Ta'ow gifting. It stood alone in the darkness, a golden beacon, piercing a thick taint that threatened to swallow the world. Lucifer's Blight darkened the sky, but the cross would not be dimmed, could not be dimmed. The heaven's shook as the two warred. The earth groaned and the moon turned to blood—human blood. *So much blood*, thought Mal'ak. *But whose blood, and why?* His eyes widened, as tendrils, black as Shadow-Bind, clawed at the flames, but the harder it fought, the brighter the cross burned, feeding the flames like a bellows wind.

Mal'ak instinctively knew there was glory due, but he was not sure of how or why. The cross burned of a glory promised, but not yet realized, and there was something else. Mal'ak's eyes pinched together. No, not something . . . *someone* was hanging on that cross. His breath caught on a lump in his throat. Sorrow hung on that cross. A man of many sorrows, with enough grief to drown the world. He was covered in the Blight and cankered severely. He barely looked human. And in the midst of all this pain, Mal'ak suddenly felt it again . . . that same burning joy he did earlier, warm and expectant—*determined*. The emotion seemed to burn as hot as the cross . . . even hotter. "What kind of joy is this?" said Mal'ak, in breathless wonder. What kind of joy, counts it a blessing to suffer? And all at once, Mal'ak knew that it wasn't the cross that the Blight warred with, but the man on the cross. Mal'ak buried his face in his hands. They were shaking. "Such knowledge is too great for me, little One," he said through muffled fingers. The Child was nowhere in sight, but Mal'ak knew He was there, listening. *This looks more like sacrifice than joy*, thought Mal'ak. *How can joy ever come at such a cost?* His jaw set in a quivering line. "I don't know anything about crosses or that man and his grief either," he said, "but I *know* joy, little One. I know it like my favorite anvil. Your kingdom's foundations are forged in part from its essence, and joy *unspeakable* and full of glory is what I feel from You right now. Blight or no, You are going to save them somehow, aren't you? *That* is what this is all about, isn't it?" asked Mal'ak, in awe. Awe, for the joy set before this baby and for the cost of reckless Love that would *somehow* achieve it. His chest swelled with wonder and pride for his King. He stared up, blinking through the runnels of tear tracks etching his furry face and laughed. He laughed so hard his wounds throbbed and his sides ached. He belly laughed for pure *joy;* for Callings and Stirrings; for providence's clear hand and for so great a Love as this. He laughed for glory concealed and for glory revealed.

Oh yes . . . there *is* glory due." His head bobbed eagerly. "There is glory due!" he shouted.

CRACKOOM!

Mal'ak's eyes popped open with a start. Rain dripped from his muzzle, pooling in shallow puddles around his ankles. The familiar scent of hell-spawn filled his nostrils and Bethlehem's soil was soft under his hooves again. The Child and Mary were under him too, but the sounds of war still raged on. He looked at his hands. They were still shaking. *Maybe it was just a dream,* he thought. Deep down, he knew that it wasn't, but he almost couldn't bear the thought. The horror of the cross still burned in his head, but oddly that burning joy still nestled close to his heart as well. He tried blinking the cross away, but the image still covered everywhere he looked. He tugged at his bushy chin. He did it so often, it was a wonder he'd not pulled a clump of it loose by now. *How long had the Child held him in the dream?*

Mal'ak licked his lips. War had a taste all its own, the stench of the dead, somehow mingled with the howls of the dying. It coated his mouth with a metallic tang that turned his stomach. *CRACKOOOM!*

Another clap struck. Instinctively, Mal'ak hovered closer to the Child and Mary. This one rung his ears, and shook the ground like the heavens were breaking. Water poured from the sky, faster than any rainstorm could muster, and without a single cloud. It doused the warding wall of flame the General had formed around them like a candle.

"Anathema!" Mal'ak blurted. Normally, he would not use words like that, but the Chronicler's words were the only ones that seem to fit the moment. Even through the deluge, Mal'ak could see the Citadel Ring standing just above where the clouds should have been. It was sundered—all of it. The Bullwarks, with its ancient walls and parapets that had withstood ten thousand battles and whose hallowed halls had been home for the High-Bourne since the fall of man, lay in ruins. Water not of earth fell from its crevices. Living water, drawn from sacred cisterns, poured onto the fallen planet unfettered. Mal'ak looked at the water, then down at the Child, brown-eyed and dimple cheeked, holding a piece of God's name in His tiny hands—a piece of His own name. The Tetragrammaton hummed to Him, shimmering like liquid.

"It's the *Child*," said Mal'ak. "I don't think He *needs* our protection," he said, now more aware than ever that he held the Great Lord himself in his arms. "He's calling the waters, and they come. The amulet is *changing* too."

"Aye," came the General's deep rasp. "He's going to change the world . . . ."

"Dawn's Light!" Mal'ak nearly jumped out of his skin. The General's voice had not come through the link, it boomed right behind him. Mal'ak turned and came almost eye to eye with the Dragon lord himself. In fact, Lucifer lay almost on top of him, and the General was on top of Lucifer. Apparently, between the carnage of battle, and the breaking of the Citadel Ring, Mal'ak had somehow missed the part where the Dragon lord had been smacked halfway across the length of the battlefield. It was a little hard to see with Light-Bringer standing between them, buried halfway to the hilt. But by the look of it, the General had managed to tackle the archdemon, pinning him in a scissor lock with his legs and wings. Mal'ak's chin dropped. Was there a Precept that covered *Dragon* tackling? Knowing the General, he would probably want to add this to his training, now that it had been done so thoroughly. Mal'ak groaned. He wasn't keen on tackling a Dragon anytime soon. Or ever, for that matter.

As Gabriel's song filled the night, Mal'ak sat wide mouthed, listening and watching as Living water poured from the Citadel Ring, flooding the battlefield called Bethlehem. To hell-spawn, it might as well have been acid. Those who did not escape were burning and in full retreat. Some of the lesser caste had turned to ash on the spot, already claimed by Baal-Shadow. And of course, there *he* stood, the General, all bristled wings and stone muscle, holding the Dragon lord in his bare hands. He was dripping wet, and wearing a grin that could only be described as bared teeth, in what was undoubtedly meant as a smile.

Dawn's Light, he's actually enjoying this, thought Mal'ak.

✳✳

The sharp cracking of his own scales giving way almost drowned out the chaos around him. The High-Bourne had started a new song, but Lucifer had bigger worries than that right now. He strained desperately to keep his eyes shut, but slowly, underneath immense pressure, the General's wings cut into him. *Shunk!* A bladed ember from the General's wings broke through, sinking a full hand-breadth into Lucifer's neck.

Pain drove Lucifer's eyes wide open and they fell directly upon that dreaded blade.

Imrah Light-Bringer blazed wildly, mere inches from his face. This time, six words pulsed on its fiery surface.

Lucifer read, then screamed in agony as the entire host of heaven rose in a crescendo, shouting in unison with his own thoughts, "GLORY TO GOD IN THE HIGHEST!" The verbal assault blew back scores of demons.

Seven Seraphim alighted around the Child, wheels spinning, latticed with lightning. Suddenly, Light-Bringer let out a roar of flame shaped like a hungry lion that threatened to consume them all. The Seraphim covered their eyes and bowed at the feet of the Child in little Mary's arms, touching their faces to the ground.

Mal'ak trembled . . . he had gotten to see a Lion after all. Maybe not an earth lion, but the Lion of the Lord of Hosts. And in that moment, Mal'ak's heart almost failed him. Lucifer lurched away, but the General's arms were unyielding. More and more High-Bourne joined in the song. Lucifer closed the flaps of his ears, trying to shut it out, but the High-Bourne kept shouting and singing, "Glory to God in the highest! Glory to God in the highest!" as the Seraphim spun their wheels faster and faster. The Elders, the Powers, and Living Creatures, all of heaven shouted with them, lending their voices with victory shouts through Gabriel's song. The sheer sound of their praise was like a sonic flood, but the meaning cut Lucifer all the more.

Merely six words, that's all it took for the Word of God to lay Lucifer open to the core. He could feel it working, quick and powerful, sharper than any two edged sword, piercing even to the dividing asunder of soul and spirit. Then, without warning, the General removed the blade from in front of his face, and gazing back at him were the ancient eyes of a timeless soul: God new—God young—but God nonetheless. Lucifer was staring into the eyes of an awakened God Child. Truth invaded his mind while the light of revelation lit his eyes.

He understood. He had been allowed to look upon

the Holy Child. No . . . he had been *made* to behold God's champion for himself. Lucifer knew of his defeat foretold in the sacred scriptures, the Word of God. But now . . . *that* Word was made flesh. His ruin was now made of man-flesh. The very stuff he had tormented for thousands of years would now be his undoing. For the first time in his long existence, Lucifer stood face to face with his own damnation, and His name . . . was Jesus.

The Beginning.

EPILOGUE

Lucifer clawed at the ground, trying to gain purchase, some sense of footing—anything at this point, but the General's arms would not budge. Without warning, the High-Bourne's iron grip loosed itself and the cool flow of shadow seeped from Lucifer's broken horn. He called to it, drawing hard upon the dark gift, and once more the slithering tendrils of night eagerly embraced him. As the darkness of Shadow-Bind swallowed him, Lucifer slowly sank into the belly of the earth, retreating to the realm of Baal-Shadow, away from the General, away from the High-

Bourne tribes, and far, far away from the Holy Child. *That was personal*, he thought, as he glided through the upper terraces of Baal-Shadow as fast as he could. The darkness deepened as he descended, but his eyes were accustomed to the dark realm. *Sheol's flames, that was a face to face challenge*, he snarled. Exhaling his frustration in a thin trail of smoke, he drummed the air with his wings then glided in silence, pondering the beating he had just endured in Bethlehem. It was no small wonder that his black heart throbbed with hate almost as much as it did with pain. Already, his mind was bent toward it—toward revenge. *Oh*, how he ached for it. Eyes glazing at that thought, he let his hatred simmer as he passed through the familiar dark of Baal-Shadow. Banking sharply, he lit upon the narrow ledge of a high-walled pit. A clutch of demons from the lesser caste huddled around a black clot of shadow bound to an altar of tenebrous stone, the only stone common in the dark realm. At his approach, they scurried like blowflies from a dead carcass. The ones without wings tried hasty bows while the others crawled on their bellies, backing out of his presence and groveling, "My looord, my looord. Hail to the Dragon lord!"

Still others just ran. And none, not one, raised their eyes to meet his. His mood was foul. There would be no dispensation, and of course, *never* mercy, and they knew it. Lucifer glided from the ledge to bottom of the pit in a single cat-like motion. Spreading his wings, he gave five giant flaps, swatting away the rest of the Legion feeding on the clotted body that was bound to the altar. That was the only reason they had not noticed his approach. "Leave me," he hissed, the air quavering with hellfire around his maw. "Have they forgotten?" he said to the altar, eyeing the body tied to it like a sparrow regarding a plump worm. "Have they forgotten that *I* and *only* I was framed from the full pattern? There is *none* . . . like . . . me," he said, standing over the body, prostrated flat against the stone. The figure was face down, clotted in Shadow-Bind just as he had left it—well, almost. The arms and legs were twisted beneath the viscous lump in unnatural angles, but the rise and fall of her breathing, told that she still held to life and the Silver Cord.

"Do they not know that I will find a way?" he whispered, bending closer to her, contempt wrinkling his muzzle and baring his teeth. "I *always* find a way . . . isn't that right, Elisssheba?" he said, smoothing her matted hair back to reveal the ageless face of the High-Bourne Captain. Her ears were gnawed off and her eye sockets were dark pools of Shadow-Bind. She was unconscious, but he continued anyway. "Have they been playing with you too hard?" He chortled a low growl, petting her head like an animal. "So . . . a Holy Child, is it?" he hissed, clicking two long talons around her slender face, whipping her head to meet his. "A child born for the feast, I say." Slowly, his lips curled back in a vicious smile as Shadow-Bind ran from her eyes in black runnels down her cheeks.

Lucifer giggled with the voice of a child, whispering into the cold dark, "I ruined the first Adam, and I will defile this baby's flesh and feed on its decay. I will find what is rotten inside of it, and nurture it." He laughed among the nameless whispers of Baal-Shadow, then stooped his broad head low, over her gnarled ear and screamed, "I will tear its flesh and drink my fill of its blood!"

All of a sudden, Lucifer doubled over. Searing pain spread across the back of his head and he groaned. Apparently the God-Flow's effects still lingered on him. Most of the pain had subsided except for a dull ache and a nagging itch at the back of his skull where Light-Bringer had struck him. Absentmindedly, he soothed the back of his head and his hand froze. Wincing, he let his claws fall into grooves that felt as if they had been burned right into his scales. He grunted, touching the deep channels carved into the back of his head. Sheol's flames, it was sore to the touch. *What now?* he asked himself. What could have left a mark on him, as surely as this?

The battle at Bethlehem lingered in his mind. The details came back to him like a cruel dream. He growled, remembering the General hitting him on the back of the skull, harder than he could ever remember being hit before.

He remembered the excruciating contact with Light-Bringer, and recalled how the General paused just before plunging the blade in front of his face, pausing as if to examine . . .

Lucifer's eyes rounded into large black orbs. His mouth fell slack, and his hands trembled, fingering what he now realized to be letters imbedded on the back of his head. Slowly, he felt along the outline of crenulated scales, his claws rising and falling with the hewn out curve of the script.

"No. No!" he howled, his hatred echoing through the corridors of Baal-Shadow, as he traced out six words branded into the back of his skull.

Glory to God in the Highest.

ABOUT THE AUTHOR

Wes Willett was born in Cherry Point, NC. He loves theology, writing, music, and is fond of most things fantasy or superhero related. He was drawn to music early in childhood. At the age of only 13, opportunity came knocking. Wes answered the call by climbing onto a bus that took him all over the country and eventually around the world, following his passion of music. He still has no idea how he convinced his parents to let him travel like this, but he's thankful, and delightfully blames his sense of adventure on his parents' lack of better judgement.

"Globetrotting will effect you," says Wes. "It's the best classroom available for perspective, especially when you're young. I think every kid should experience a missions trip." He explains (with a straight face,) "When I was a kid, I was on track to become the very first singing-Jedi Knight-bass player, but apparently, God had a different path for me. The path of the worship pastor that loves to write. "Believe me," he says, rolling his eyes, "I'm as surprised as anyone..."

Wes has been writing, playing bass and singing with artists such as:

Michael Boggs, Anthony Evans, Chris Rice, CeCe Winans and many more.

He currently enjoys playing bass for Travis Cottrell at the Living Proof Live, Beth Moore events. You can follow his schedule at theinkforge.com.

Wes is the worship pastor of TSC, South Campus, in Columbia, TN, where he resides with his beautiful wife and daughter.

GLOSSARY

Adam

1. The first of the sons of clay.

2. He who was given dominion of earth by God.

3. The first human.

Ages

1. An order of time beyond what humans understand of their existing chronology.

2. The celestial dispensations of time in direct connection with the Quintessence. (*see Quintessence*)

(Note): Gabriel the archangel is the Chronicler of these Ages. (*see Chronicler*)

Age of the Turning

1. When Lucifer abused the Great Song of Songs to try and steal the Great Lord's glory.

2. The first and greatest battle creation has ever known.

3. When Lucifer the Dragon lord and the Legion were cast from Heaven by Michael and the High-Bourne tribes.

Aspects

1. The ancients that rule the deep black seas of a realm called the Narrows.

2. Mysterious creatures that predate angels.

Baal-Shadow ('bā(ə)l shadow)

1. A mysterious realm cloaked in darkness. It is composed in part, of living shadow, and the essence of disembodied demon remains.

2. Where demons go and what they become when they die.

(*see Shadow-Bind*)

Blight of the World (blīt)

1. A curse Lucifer unleashed upon humans through Adam and Eve's sin.

2. The curse which Samyaza bonded with to become Death.

3. Sin.

(*see Samyaza*)

Cherub ('ch erəb)

1. An angelic being depicted in ancient history as part bull, lion, eagle, and human, having wings and holding rank as the second highest order of the celestial ninefold hierarchy.

Chronicler

1. The Archangel known as Gabriel. An angel of unique calling among the High-Bourne tribes, set apart by his knowledge and use of the ancient musical language called the Old Tongue. (*see Old Tongue*)

2. The Great Lord's bard, historian, and messenger.

Citadel Ring

1. The Cloud City

2. A floating network of fortresses encompassing the world of humans.

3. Where High-Bourne angels live and dwell.

Cipher ('sīfər)

1. A secret way of writing or speaking.

2. A code.

3. The Old Tongue is hidden within the "cipher" of a divine song called the Song of Songs. (*see Song of Songs*)

Daq (dok)

1. Crafters native to the northern mountains of the Narrows. (*see Narrows*)

2. The small statured folk of the Realm of the Aspects.

EliSheba (el-ee-sheh'-bah)

1. A female High-Bourne, and servant of He Who Brings the Dawn.

2. Protector of the Seven Seals.

3. The Chronicler's heir and apprentice.

Essence

1. That which flows inside the celestial caste.

2. The equivalent of blood, for a spirit being.

Eve

1. The first of the daughters of clay.

2. She who was given dominion of earth.

3. The first woman.

Flesh-Walkers

1. A term spirit beings use to refer to Adam and Eve's children.

2. Humans.

Forge-Crafting

1. A forging process perfected by Crafters enabling them to give shape to the words of God.

2. A permanent way of forging an utterance of the Old Tongue within an object, essentially infusing the power of a God Word within an object forever.

3. Giving shape to the words of God.

(*see Old Tongue*)

The General

1. Michael the archangel.

2. Archistrategos, general of the earthbound war tribes of angels known as the High-Bourne.

(see *High-Bourne*)

Grigori

1. A group of demons separate from the Legion who broke the Prime Command of the Great Lord and were imprisoned for all time in the realm of Baal-Shadow for their trespass.

2. Those demons responsible for the Nephilim who walk the earth.

3. The Fallen.

Half-Life

1. A manifestation of human anguish given life.

2. A construct of human anguish made tangible and animated by the power of the Tome of Maleficus.

(see *Tome of Maleficus, Wyrm*)

High-Bourne (Shade of His Hand)

1. The war tribes of angelic beings left on the earth after the Age of the Turning, when Lucifer defied God and was cast out. (*see Age of the Turning*)

2. Guardian Angels.

Imrah (The Lightbringer)

1. A two edged sword, carried by the General.

2. The Word of God canonized on a blade, forged from light, and tempered seven times within the wheel of a Seraph's heart.

Kolossos

1. One of the larger demons within ranks of the Legion.

2. A huge horned demon.

Legion

1. The third part of heaven that followed Lucifer the Dragon lord at the Age of the Turning, when he defied the Great Lord and was cast to earth.

2. Fallen Angels.

3. Demons.

Leviathan (The Shadow of the Deep)

1. One of four Aspects.

2. One of the four keepers of the Tetragrammaton.

3. A celestial caste that predates angels and demons.

(*see Aspects, Tetragrammaton*)

Lucifer

1. The leader of the group demons known as the Legion.

2. The demon who brought forth the curse of the Blight (sin) upon humans.

3. The Dragon lord.

(*see Blight*)

Mal'ak (mal-awk')

1. A Bovine faced angel of the High-Bourne tribes.

2. The only High-Bourne without wings.

3. The only High-Bourne whose calling is Sacrosanct.

Mawgore

1. A savage pit hound of the Legion.

2. These demons travel in packs and feed upon fear.

Narrows (Realm of the Aspects)

1. A vast magical sea, out of phase with earth time, known as the Deep of the Narrows or the Realm of the Aspects.

2. Home of the Leviathan and the other Aspects.

3. The barrier between heaven and earth.

Old Tongue

1. The first language spoken.

2. A divine language only ciphered through music.

3. God language; the language He used to create the universe, and the source of magic.

(*see Cipher, Rune-Crafting, Forge-Crafting*)

Onyia

1. One of the enchanted ships known as Sea Stryders.

(*see Sea Stryders*)

Oracle

1. A rare object that has been power-wrought in the divine language of the Old Tongue through Forge-Crafting.
(*see Forge-Crafting*)

2. An object capable of channeling an utterance of the God-Flow.

Prime Command

1. A law set in place by the Great Lord that insures that humans have the right to a free will choice.

2. A law that also demands that the High-Bourne of the Great Lord must preserve faith at all costs. Specifically, human faith.

3. It is the reason Angels and Demons do not reveal or show themselves to humans.

Quintessence (kwin'tesəns)

1. A fifth element.

2. A divine law that taps into the numerical properties latent in all things and the medium through which a divine sequence of numbers correlate with, and alter the lines of probability, allowing the impossible to happen.

3. The formula for a miracle.

Rune-Crafting

1. An utterance of the Old Tongue inscribed upon something or someone.

2. A temporary inscribing or speaking a single word or portion of a word from the Old Tongue to create various Wards for protection, healing, and combat etc...

3. Written Magic.

(*see Forge-Crafting*)

Samyaza

1. The lord of Baal-Shadow. A demon that bonded with the curse of sin called the Blight and in so doing, was transformed into the embodiment of Death.

2. Leader of a powerful group of demons called the Grigori. (*see Grigori*)

3. The death angel.

Seal

1. Seals were brought forth at the Age of the Turning, crafted from high magic to protect or imprison something.

2. Magic that cannot be broken by anything save death.

Sea Stryders

1. Enchanted wooden ships, native to the dark waters of the Narrows

2. The ships responsible for bringing the High-Bourne to the Haze of earth.

Seraphim ('serə‚fim)

1. An angelic being, of the highest order of the ninefold celestial hierarchy.

Shadow-Bind

1. Demon Magic.

2. The power to bind Baal-Shadow to ones will.

(*see Baal-Shadow*)

3. The ability to call on the darkness and traverse its realms.

Shamayin (shaw-mah'-yin)

1. An ancient weapon crafted before the Age of the Turning.

2. The Fist of Heaven.

Sheol (ˈsh ē ͵ôl)

1. The underworld, dwelling place of the dead.

2. Where the Lake of Fire burns eternal.

Song of Songs

(*see Old Tongue*)

Summoning Stones

1. Oracles that are portals to and from the Narrows.

(*see Narrows, Oracle*)

Tachan

1. A High-Bourne angel.

Tannin

1. A Dragon lord in the ranks of the Legion.

2. A large golden Dragon.

Ta'ow

1. The bull-faced and cloven footed angels of the Ta'ow tribes.

2. The Crafters, Forgers, and Builders of the heavenly caste.

Tetragrammaton

1. Four sacred Oracles, each holding a single utterance of the divine name.

2. The name of God.

The God-Flow

1. The torrential flow of energy that spins galaxies and beats the hearts of men into life inside the womb.
(*see The Silver Cord*)

2. The binding authority by which creation remains and consists.

The Silver Cord

1. The lifeline through which flows the quickening power of the God-Flow and that which tethers all sentient beings, past, present and future to the Great Lord Almighty.

Tome of Maleficus (Lucifer's Book)

1. The Book of Lucifer.

2. A book who's power is tied to both the spirit world and physical world by a blood tether (sacrifice).

3. It can give shape to the anguish of mankind in the form of Constructs.

Trogs

1. A Legion demon of the smaller caste. Trogs travel in huge swarms with speed and agility that more than make up for their small stature. Built for the kill, they have talons for hands and feet and hole shaped mouths for boring inside of their prey.

Ward

1. A temporary rune of magic that has been inscribed upon an object or someone.

Wyrm (worm) (half-life)

1. A parasitic creature not really alive, but not really dead.
2. A construct animated by the power of the Tome of Maleficus.

(*see Tome of Maleficus*)

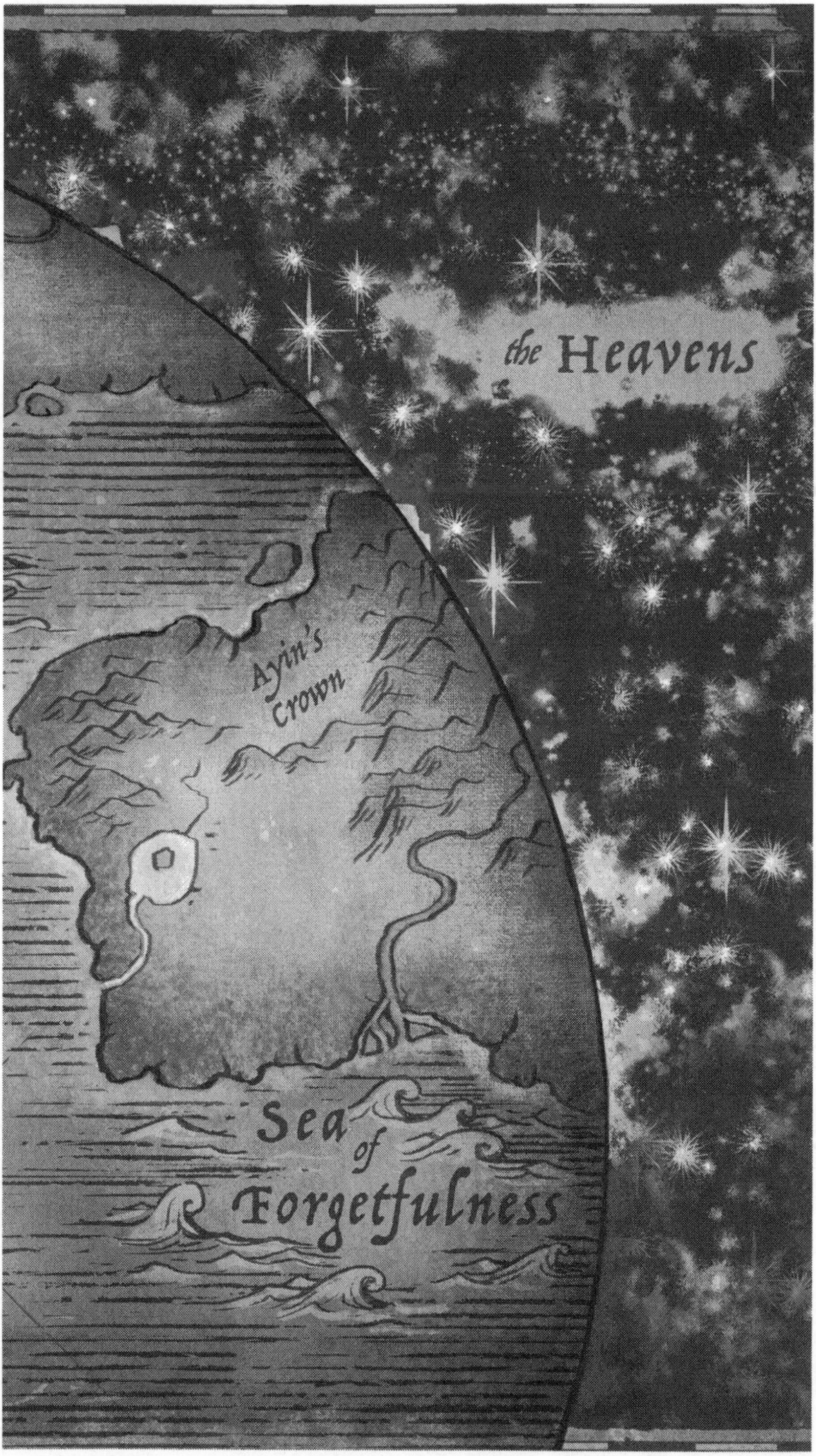
the Heavens
Ayin's Crown
Sea of Forgetfulness